CH00895044

Cambridge Libraries, Archives and Information Service

This book is due for return on or before the latest date shown above, but may be renewed up to three times unless it has been requested by another customer.

Books can be renewed - in person at your local library

Cambridgeshire County Council

Online www.cambridgeshire.gov.uk/library

Please note that charges are made on overdue books.

books is a treat worth savouring."
Jo at Jaffareadstoo

Praise for *The Man in the Canary Waistcoat*

"Having read the first Sam Plank novel and really enjoyed it I was so looking forward to the next, and 'The Man in the Canary Waistcoat' did not disappoint. Susan Grossey is an excellent storyteller. The descriptions of Regency London are vivid and create a real sense of time and place. Sam Plank, Martha and Wilson are great characters – well-drawn and totally individual in their creation. The dialogue is believable and the pace well fitted to this genre. The novel shows excellent research and writing ability – a recommended read."
Barbara Goldie, The Kindle Book Review

"Regency police constable Sam Plank, so well established in the first book, continues to develop here, with an interesting back story emerging about his boyhood, which shapes his attitude to crime as an adult. Like the first book, this is not so much a whodunit as a whydunit, and Grossey skilfully unfolds a complex tale of financial crime and corruption. There are fascinating details about daily life in the criminal world woven into the story, leaving the reader much more knowledgeable without feeling that he's had a history lesson."
Debbie Young, author and book blogger

Praise for *Worm in the Blossom*

"Ever since I was introduced to Constable Sam Plank
and his intrepid wife Martha, I have followed his
exploits with great interest. There is something so
entirely dependable about Sam: to walk in his footsteps
through nineteenth century London is rather like being
in possession of a superior time travelling machine...
The writing is, as ever, crisp and clear, no superfluous
waffle, just good old fashioned storytelling, with a
tantalising beginning, an adventurous middle, and a
wonderfully dramatic ending."
Jo at Jaffareadstoo

"Susan Grossey not only paints a meticulous portrait of
London in this era, she also makes the reader see it on
its own terms, for example recognising which style of
carriage is the equivalent to a 21st century sports-car,
and what possessing one would say about its owner... In
short, a very satisfying and agreeable read in an addictive
series that would make a terrific Sunday evening
television drama series."
Debbie Young, author and book blogger

PORTRAITS OF PRETENCE

Susan Grossey

CreateSpace Independent
Publishing Platform

Book layout ©2016 BookDesignTemplates.com

Portraits of Pretence / Susan Grossey -- 1st edition
ISBN 978-1537430102

For Lorraine,
for her belief and pride in me
for the past thirty-nine years

The appearance of right oft leads us wrong.

—HORACE

Author's note

Any period of history has its own vocabulary, both standard and slang. The Regency was no different, and in order to capture the spirit of the time I have used words and phrases that may not be familiar to the modern reader. At the end of this book there is a glossary of these terms and their brief definitions.

CHAPTER ONE

The charming Elizabeth

MONDAY 8ᵀᴴ JANUARY 1827

Wilson rubbed his shoulder as he held the door, now hanging off one of its hinges, aside for me.

"Dear heavens," he said behind me. "No wonder the old girl was complaining."

From the foot of the stairs we could hear the landlady calling up to us. "What is it? Can you see? Is he there?"

"Wait down there, Mrs Anderson," said Wilson. He looked over the banisters. "A warm drink would go down well, if you're asking." A few moments later I could hear her in the kitchen below us.

Wilson and I stepped into the dingy room and peered into the darkness. Holding my arm across my nose I walked to the small window and, with my free hand, pushed open the shutters with a bang. I gulped in the cold air; it was far from fresh but a sight better than the fetid atmosphere in that squalid room. In the dim light now cast across the floor, we could see all the signs of a struggle: the two chairs were both upturned, one missing a leg, and the floor was covered with whatever had once been on the table – smashed pots, torn scraps of paper, and several pens. I bent and picked one up. Not pens: paintbrushes, with fine, pointed hairs for close work. Wilson crouched down next to what looked like a jumble of old clothes but which, on closer inspection, proved to be rather more.

"This must be him," he said. He picked up the man's wrist, as I had taught him, and felt for the pulse. "Nothing," he said sadly, and gently laid down the arm again. "Several days ago, judging from the smell."

I heard the stairs creak, and turned around to see Mrs Anderson at the door, a tray in her hands. Wilson made as though to shield the body.

"Don't you worry about my finer feelings, young man," said the landlady. "You don't keep a house in this part of town for as many years as I have without seeing a few gone to meet their Maker." She looked about the room. "But this one didn't go easy, did he?"

I reached for one of the cups and shook my head. "Did you not hear anything – raised voices? The furniture?" I indicated the broken chair.

"I was away for two days, visiting my sister in Bromley. When I came back I didn't see him, but then that was nothing unusual – kept odd hours, he did."

I held out the paintbrush. "An artist, was he?"

"So he said," she replied with a sniff, "but I had my doubts. Not proper paintings, anyway. Tiny little things, they were – couldn't hardly see them. No bigger than the palm of your hand."

"Miniatures?" I asked. She shrugged.

"Like this, sir," said Wilson. He walked over and handed me a small oval. "I was checking the body and it was in his other hand – clutched tight. He didn't want them to take it, whoever they were."

I walked over to the window and held the oval to the light. It was one of the loveliest things I had ever seen. Only about two inches high and less than that wide, it was a tiny portrait of a little girl. Aged about five, she smiled shyly out at me in her finest dress with a silk sash at the waist, her cheeks rosy and her eyes bright blue. She was enchanting. Wilson stood at my shoulder.

"She's a pretty thing," he said. "Daughter?" He jerked his head towards the dead man. "Or grand-daughter, more like?"

"Possibly," I said. "Or maybe a valuable commission that he did not want to lose."

I walked to the door and showed the portrait to Mrs Anderson. She shook her head. "Never seen her," she said. "He didn't have many callers."

"Family?" I asked.

She shook her head again. "Nice and quiet, he was. Mind you, he didn't speak much English, so that helped." I raised my eyebrows. "French," she elaborated. "Mr Rambert. Turned up one day, oh, about four years ago now, with another man – he was English, that one," she nodded at me, "and paid a month in advance. They liked the room because of the window – good light, they said. After that he," she pointed to the man on the floor, "Mr Rambert, paid himself. Every Friday, regular as clockwork. I wish all my tenants were as reliable."

"Did the Englishman come back?"

"Not that I saw, no. But then I'm not always here, as I said," she replied.

"Can you remember anything about him?" I asked.

The landlady thought for a moment. "He was about your age. Bit taller than you, but not as tall as him." She pointed at Wilson.

"Whoever that little girl was, she meant a great deal to him," said Wilson. He bent down and turned over the man's hand to show me: Rambert had grasped the miniature so tightly that the metal frame had bitten into his skin and drawn blood.

"Well, it worked," I said, "Whoever did this to him missed it." I took out my handkerchief and wrapped it around the portrait before slipping it into my coat pocket. "Once Constable Wilson and I have finished looking around the room," I said to Mrs Anderson, putting my cup back on the tray, "we will return to the police office and arrange for an undertaker to come and take the body. We might send someone else to see the room, so don't touch anything or clean it until I send word. And if anyone comes calling, asking for our late friend, say that you don't know what has happened to him and then send word to me – Constable Sam Plank, at Great Marlborough Street."

Mr Conant sighed as he held the miniature to the light from the window.

"Charming, isn't she?" he asked and I nodded. "I'm no expert, but this looks like fine work to me. See, here." I walked over to him and he turned the portrait so that I could see it. "Take the glass and look at her sash, there, where it casts a shadow on her skirt." I took the magnifier from him and looked; the two fabrics seemed real enough to touch. "They say that the best artists use a brush with a single hair," he mused, shaking his head in wonder. "The patience they must have – the steadiness of hand. Rambert, you say?"

The magistrate took the glass back from me and laid it and the miniature carefully on his desk.

"That's what the landlady said," I replied.

"Rambert," repeated Conant. "Not a name I know but then, as I say, I'm no expert. But I know someone who is – something of a collector of miniatures himself, and a dealer in curiosities. Henri Causon. His premises are not far from here – Maddox Street, I believe. Perhaps you could call on him with our young lady and see what he can tell you. If Mr Rambert is responsible for this, then it is sad to see the death of such a talented artist. Those cheeks – you could fairly pinch them, couldn't you?"

"Ivory?" asked Martha. "From an elephant?" She put her hand to the side of the pot to check that it was warming and then came to sit opposite me at the table.

"That's what Mr Conant said," I replied. "They take the tusk of the elephant and cut layers from the outside, then polish them and paint on them. I tell you, Martha," I leaned back in my chair, "it makes the skin on that little girl's face look alive – warm. Glowing. I've never seen anything like it. Look."

"You have it here?" said my wife as I put my hand into my pocket.

I nodded, laying the little bundle on the table and carefully unfolding the napkins that Conant had lent me. "Mr Conant wants me to visit a curiosity dealer he knows, who may be able to tell us more about the artist. And perhaps about her." I picked up the miniature and handed it to Martha. She carefully wiped her hands on her apron before reaching out for the tiny thing.

She gazed at the miniature for a long minute. "The pictures I've seen before now," she said, "well, apart from the ones in churches, of course – the ones of people, I mean..."

"Portraits," I suggested. "Portraits on canvas."

"Yes. Well, they always look a bit stiff. Not – glowing, as you say."

"That's the beauty of the ivory. But you can only use it for miniatures because it comes in small pieces."

"And you think this Mr Rambert painted her?" asked my wife.

"He was definitely a painter; the room was full of paints and brushes. But there were no other pictures, and no more pieces of ivory. Just this one, which we think they overlooked. It's all we have at the moment."

"Elizabeth," said Martha quietly. "Do you not think she looks like an Elizabeth?"

"Perhaps," I replied with a gentle smile. "Wilson thinks she may be the artist's grand-daughter – he was old enough. It would explain why he was so reluctant to let her go." I waited for a moment. "As are you, it would seem," I said, holding out my hand.

Martha took one more look at the miniature, sighed softly and then handed it back to me. She stood and went to the stove, stirring the stew before raising the spoon to her lips to blow on it and taste. I wrapped the miniature in the protective napkins once more and returned it to my pocket. Martha put two plates onto the table and ladled out the stew; I reached for my steaming dish and then paused, as Martha had known I would. She rolled her eyes and added two more potatoes.

"Mr Rambert must have been a famous artist," my wife said as she sat down with her own plate, "for them to go to all that trouble to steal his work."

"You think he was targeted?" I asked.

"Well, it certainly wasn't a random attack, was it? Not in the man's room, on the third floor of a lodging house? No, his attackers went to find him, or followed him there. He was the one they were after."

"I shall have to be careful you don't take my job," I said, "with astute observations like that."

My wife looked at me with a smile. "After twenty-five years, it would be a pretty poor constable's wife who didn't learn to notice everything," she said.

CHAPTER TWO

The curiosity dealer

TUESDAY 9TH JANUARY 1827 – MORNING

"Twenty-five years!" said Wilson as we walked along Great Portland Street the next morning.

"Longer than you've been alive," I said.

He shook his head wonderingly. "A quarter century." Such expanses of time seem unimaginable to the young. "How did you meet Mrs Plank?" he asked.

"All those years ago now," I said, "I can barely remember." But that was not true: I could remember every detail. "Mrs Plank's father was an innkeeper – a rough place in Holborn. Laystall Street." Wilson nodded. "I was walking past one evening and a little girl was sitting on the step crying. I stopped to ask what was the matter and she said that her sister had scolded her. Just then the scolding sister came out with a piece of barley sugar by way of apology. That was Martha – Mrs Plank." With curls that could not be tamed, skin like buttermilk, and deep brown eyes that undid me the moment I saw them. "She thanked me for comforting the little one, we fell to talking, I happened to walk down that same street the next evening, and the next, and two years later we were married."

"So if you hadn't gone that way that evening, or if Mrs Plank hadn't scolded her sister, you would never have met and she would have married someone else," said Wilson as we turned into Great Marlborough Street.

"I was a handsome young fellow of twenty, with a bit of ambition about me," I said. "She was lucky to find me still on the market." But we both knew that I was blustering: when it came to luck and our marriage, it was all on my side, and many's the time I have thanked whatever impulse pushed me to walk down Laystall Street that long-ago evening.

As misfortune would have it, there were warrants aplenty that day, and it was not until late in the afternoon that I could attend to the miniature. The brass plaque by the door of number 9 Maddox Street confirmed it to be the premises of Henri Causon, curiosity dealer. I put my hand to my pocket as I had already done a dozen times that day, to check that Elizabeth was still there, and then knocked. A maid came to the door and I explained who I was and that I wished to see her master on a matter of business, on the recommendation of John Conant Esquire. She took my hat and showed me to a small parlour, saying that she would tell Mr Causon of my arrival.

The curiosity dealer certainly practised what he preached. In the room where I waited, every surface was covered with ornaments, statuettes, gilt boxes and coins, while the walls displayed drawings and paintings of every size, from grand landscapes to tiny, intimate sketches. There was even a pair of miniature portraits side by side near the mantelpiece and I was just walking over to examine them when the door opened and the maid said that Mr Causon would receive me in the drawing room.

In his sombre black jacket and snowy cravat, Henri Causon stood in sharp contrast to the profusion of colour and excess in his drawing room, which was even more filled with examples of his trade than the parlour I had just left. He was a tall man with defined features, in particular a long, straight nose down which he looked at me now. He came toward me and bowed before putting out his hand.

"After many years in your fine city, Constable Plank, I have learned how the Englishman does love to shake hands. With this firm grip, you can tell that I am a man to be trusted, no?"

"I can tell that you are a man not armed with a sword," I replied.

"Which is also useful to know," he said with a smile. "Come: you will join me in a little cognac before we turn to business." It was a statement rather than a question, and I took a seat on the small sofa that he indicated. He poured two measures from a decanter and handed one to me.

"To your health, and to my santé," he said and raised his glass. I did likewise. It was an uncommonly fine wine and I looked at him in appreciation. "All duty paid," he said with a wink. "One of the many benefits of the re-newed friendship between our two countries."

"You say that you have lived in London for many years," I prompted.

"Many," he replied. "My late wife and I came here at the end of the last century, as did plenty of our country-men." I nodded: London had provided sanctuary to many who had fallen foul of the new regime in France. "We were young then, of course – all of us." He smiled at me. "My wife died nearly twenty years ago now, and my son returned to France. He was a babe in arms when we came to London, but he always said he felt more French. And he died for her, for France. Leipzig." I said nothing: what is there to say to a man who has lost a son? He was silent for a moment or two and then seemed to remember me. "I, on the other hand, well, there is little for me now in France, and so I stay. My daughter and I, we stay."

His mention of a daughter brought Elizabeth to mind and I put my hand to my pocket. Causon saw the movement and put down his glass.

"Ah, you have something to show me," he said. He leaned towards me and I handed him the miniature. He carefully unwrapped the cloth and held the portrait in the flat of one hand while reaching into his pocket with the other, bringing out a small oval mother-of-pearl case. He passed it to me.

"Would you open that for me, please?" he said.

I pushed the side of the case and a magnifying lens swung out. "A neat device," I said, handing it back to him, but his attention was elsewhere. He bent forward and looked closely at the miniature, moving the magnifier across it as he examined the picture itself, the frame and even the reverse. I waited.

"Exquisite," he said finally, still looking through the magnifier. "The finest quality. Where did you obtain it?" I said nothing, and he looked up at me, blinking. "I see, I see. Still, no matter. You have come to me for a professional appraisal and this I can offer."

I took my notebook out of my pocket. "Do you mind?" I asked. "The memory is not always reliable."

"It fades, does it not, constable? The memory, the eyesight," he waved the magnifier at me. "It all fades. By all means, take your notes." His voice became business-like in tone. "Miniature three-quarter portrait of female child in formal wear and setting. Watercolour on ivory. Unknown sitter and unknown artist – which does not mean that we shall never know, constable, but simply that the work is unsigned. Estimated date – I shall say 1800, from the look of the frame, and the way the little girl's hair is curled. I cannot be sure, but I would guess that it was painted ad vivum – from life, that is – or at the very least by someone who knew the child well. The – how to put this? – the emotion of the piece would not be present in a mere copy."

I looked up from my notebook and nodded. "I felt that too – and my wife. She has taken to calling her Elizabeth." I flushed slightly.

"Hah!" My host smiled. "Your wife is a woman of feeling. Elizabeth: it suits her, I think, and will work as well in French as in English." He took another close look at the miniature. "Yes, she is definitely French, our little Elizabeth."

"We can't keep it, you know, my love," I said as Martha carefully placed the wrapped miniature in the top drawer of the dresser and patted it before hiding it away.

"Of course I know that, Sam," she said, "but I am enjoying having something so lovely to look at." She lifted the cloth covering a bowl of potatoes and counted some out before glancing at Wilson and adding another one.

"Ten guineas," she said, shaking her head. "Imagine something so tiny being worth so much."

"Mr Causon said it was just his educated guess, and that the only way to know for certain would be to put it up for sale and see what someone is prepared to pay for it. But something like that, yes," I said. "If it were a portrait of someone well-known, and painted by a respected artist, it would be worth ten times that."

"And yet the attackers left it behind," said Martha.

"It was hidden in Rambert's hand, so they might not have known that it was there," I suggested. "Although Wilson found it quickly enough – and if they were robbers they would have gone through every last one of their victim's pockets before leaving. So if they were not looking for valuables, what were they doing?"

We sat for a moment and thought.

"Although they made a mess, as robbers would do," said Wilson after a while, "Mrs Anderson told me that nothing in particular was missing – his easel was there, and his box of paints. Quite a handsome one, too. With his name carved inside the lid: Louis Rambert."

"So not a robbery," I said. "Self-murder?"

Wilson blinked. "With those injuries?"

"Quite right. Which leaves us with…"

"Murder by another hand," said Wilson, making a note in his book. He turned back a few pages. "I went to see the body at the undertaker's, like you said, once it was cleaned up, and he'd had a good beating. But he was killed by a knife wound – here." Wilson pointed to just below his heart.

"But we found no knife in the room or on the body, did we?" I asked.

Wilson looked back through his notes. "Only a knife for eating," he said, "and something called a palette knife – a flat thing used for mixing paints. Nothing sharp or pointed enough for that injury."

"So why would his attackers bring a suitable knife with them, and then go to the trouble of beating Mr Rambert before stabbing him?" I asked. I had a fair idea, but simply telling Wilson would rob him of the chance to think of it for himself. "Our artist was no greenhead, was he?"

Wilson shook his head, running his finger down a page of notes. "No: the undertaker thought he looked about sixty-five."

"So…"

"So unlikely to have put up much of a fight – the attackers could have just killed him outright." Wilson paused. "Perhaps they beat him to throw us off the scent – to make it look like a bungled robbery or a matter of business gone wrong. When all along it was a planned murder." He looked up at me with eagerness. I nodded, and a wide grin spread across his face until he remembered that he was supposed to be a seasoned constable.

He cleared his throat and carefully underlined the word *Murder* in his notes. Martha and I glanced at each other over his head and smiled.

CHAPTER THREE

Conant borrows
a soldier

TUESDAY 9TH JANUARY 1827 – EVENING

"Ah, good evening, constable," said Mr Conant as I knocked on the door of his dining room which had been left ajar. "I've sent Thin Billy to bed, so we'll have to shift for ourselves." He smiled at the surprise on my face. "Williams and I are well aware of what you constables call him."

The magistrate's footman was a long, lanky fellow and so the nickname was perhaps inevitable.

The clock on the mantelpiece struck the half hour and I raised my hand to cover a yawn; Martha and I had been preparing for bed when the message lad arrived with the note from Conant, and it was some time since I had found myself on duty at past midnight.

"Mrs Plank will forgive the intrusion, I hope," said Conant as he went across to the coffee pot left ready on a tray and poured two cups.

"As the wife of a constable, she is used to interrupted sleep," I said, taking a cup from the magistrate. I waited until he had settled into one of the fireside armchairs and indicated the other before seating myself.

"I considered waiting until morning, but an opportunity presented itself, and..." Conant put down his drink on the side table at his elbow and reached into his coat pocket. He took out a small bundle of linen and handed it to me. I likewise put down my cup and rested the bundle on my knees to unwrap it. At its heart was a miniature portrait in a rather ornate gold frame. Slightly larger than Elizabeth, this one was of a young adult man, with carefully curled dark hair and wearing a fine red military coat with an embroidered black collar, all against a fanciful background of rolling hills. I looked up questioningly at Conant.

"This evening I dined at the home of Lord Winstanley, a distant cousin of my late wife," he explained. "We see each other rarely, but his eldest son is to marry and there will be something of a massing of the clans. Winstanley wanted to ask whether Lily would attend as a bridesmaid." The magistrate smiled. "I said that I will put the invitation to her – that was all I could promise."

Conant's daughter Lily was a young lady of independent spirit; at times her father feigned exasperation at her unwillingness to tread the well-worn path from father's care to husband's, but his pride in her quick wit and her reluctance to settle for a quiet life were plain to all who knew him.

"After supper Winstanley took several of the gentlemen to view a collection of miniature paintings that he has gathered. Most of them were, shall we say, immodest in subject." The magistrate looked over at me and I tried to make my face as expressionless as possible. "Based on classical subjects, of course, but with a particular admiration for the female form in its most natural state."

"Indeed," I said. "But this one..." I indicated the portrait of the young man.

"As we were looking at the collection – presented in velvet trays housed in drawers in a locked cabinet – I noticed that there were about a half-dozen finer than the rest. They were more suitable for public display: portraits of fully clothed subjects," the magistrate gave a small smile, "in Arcadian landscapes. Portraits that might be offered as keepsakes or love tokens. This fellow is one of them."

"Did you ask Lord Winstanley about the sitter when you asked to borrow his portrait?" I asked.

Conant cleared his throat. "Ah, well, 'borrow' might not be strictly accurate. If my suspicion is correct – that this miniature is also the work of Rambert – then I did not want to have to explain to my host why I was so interested in it. As I helped him to replace one of the drawers in the cabinet, I took hold of the nearest portrait to me and slipped it into my cuff. And when I return it to Winstanley tomorrow – well, later today – with my most fulsome apologies, I shall explain that the twisted metal edging of the frame caught hold of the lace on my sleeve and it was not until I undressed that I discovered it."

"Which is why time is of the essence," I said.

The magistrate nodded. "I want you to take this little fellow to Causon first thing in the morning, along with the other miniature that you have still, and ask him whether, in his opinion, they are the work of the same man. If they are, it may help us to learn more about who killed Mr Rambert."

CHAPTER FOUR

Poor French widows

WEDNESDAY 10TH JANUARY 1827

After a hurried breakfast, I returned to Maddox Street. Causon was as welcoming this time as the last, and soon we were leaning over a small table by the window, where the morning light was best, looking closely at the two miniatures now laid side by side. Causon bent down, his mother-of-pearl magnifier in his hand.

"Hmmm," he said quietly to himself. "And here, too." He picked up Elizabeth and held her in the flat of his hand, looking along the length of the portrait, and then did the same with the miniature of the uniformed young man. "Yes, yes – that would be the case."

I waited in silence; breaking another man's train of thought is rarely helpful. Eventually the dealer laid down his magnifier and drew up two chairs, taking one himself and waving me into the other.

"Now, constable, I can offer no guarantees. You come to me for an opinion, yes, and this is what I give you." I nodded and took out my notebook. "Neither of these miniatures is signed, but that is not unusual for portraits of this size, this intimacy. But artists can leave a signature other than their name, as you know. An old man sitting in a darkened room, with wrinkles, a double-chin and a textured cloak about him," here Causon swirled his hand around his throat to demonstrate, "does not need a signature for us to suspect the hand of Rembrandt. And so these little ones carry the mark of their maker. First, they are both on ivory, but before ivory can be used for portraits it must be polished to a smooth surface – and the ivory in both these cases has been polished in the same manner, the same direction. So the same man prepared both pieces – either the artist himself, or his supplier. Second, the two pieces use the same palette of colours: the red of the uniform is the same as that of the little girl's sash."

"But all artists would use red," I said.

"Indeed, constable, indeed – but there is not simply one red pigment. There is brilliant crimson – carmine, they call it – and Venetian red, light red, Indian red, and more besides. And when I look through my glass at those two items of clothing, I see that they are painted using exactly the same pigment." Causon waited until I had finished writing before continuing. "And third – and for me, this is the most persuasive point – there is great similarity of technique between the two portraits. Here, let me show you." The dealer handed me his magnifier. "Look at the nose of each sitter. The very tip. What do you see?"

"Their noses?" I asked. Causon nodded, smiling eagerly like a magician about to perform a baffling trick, and I stood up and then bent low over the table, peering through the glass first at Elizabeth and then at the young man. And then I saw it: right on the tip of each nose was a minute dot of white. I looked at Causon.

"Right on the very end, no?" he said, pointing to his own nose. "Bright white – just a dab to highlight the tip. It makes the nose look more natural, less flat."

"Surely all artists will know that?" I asked, handing back the magnifier.

"Not all, no – but the more practised ones, certainly. And a dab on the end of a life-sized nose is quite simple to achieve, in normal portraiture. But a dot – a tiny, almost invisible dot – on the end of a miniature nose, well, that requires great skill and steadiness, which are altogether more rare."

"So in your opinion, sir…" I prompted.

"In my opinion, constable, your two miniatures are by the same hand."

Mr Conant shook his head in bewilderment. "I some-times wonder whether the running of this country is in the right hands. Winstanley is no scholar, to be sure – my late wife had all the brains in that family – but even for him it is quite something to boast that all of his pretty little pictures came to him by way of Cheapside! To tell me, a magistrate, that he has profited by taking advantage of poor French widows and the like, stripping them of their family treasures." Conant shook his head again and downed his drink in one. "I almost regretted returning the portrait to him, I will confess." We sat in silence for a few moments, contemplating the avarice of Lord Win-stanley. "But tell me, constable, what did our French dealer say?"

I described to the magistrate the careful examination that Causon had made of the two portraits. "To conclude, he stated that he was of the opinion that the two minia-tures – Elizabeth, and the young soldier you returned to your cousin..."

"My wife's cousin, the fool," corrected Conant.

"...to your wife's cousin today – are by the same artist. That artist, we believe, is the late Mr Rambert, who lived and worked here in London. And yet your cousin – your wife's cousin – claimed that his miniatures had been found in France?"

Conant thought for a moment. "Winstanley was def-inite. When I gave the young red-coated chap back to him and explained how I came to have it, Winstanley was almost dismissive. He said that the keepsake miniatures had been thrown in as part of the deal when he bought the other, more revealing pieces. He didn't care for them much, but he never could resist a bargain, I recall. When I enquired where he had bought them, he winked at me – odious fellow – and said that he had an agent who kept an eye out for suitable pieces for his collection, and arranged to have them brought across the Channel. A private shipment, he called it – another wink at this."

I looked at the magistrate. "So how would miniatures painted in England – right here in London – end up being brought in from France?"

"Winstanley is, as I say, a prize fool. It would be like him to believe any Banbury tale that someone might tell." Conant smiled. "I will admit I like to think of him paying over the odds for his unseemly collection."

Wilson listened carefully as I told him what Conant and I had discussed. The evening was closing in as we walked together northwards along Great Titchfield Street. It had started out as a duty for me, walking part of the way home with the young man and talking through his day's work, but I will confess that I now found it more of a pleasure than an obligation. Wilson was growing into a fine constable, with an enquiring mind and a careful logic.

"Perhaps Rambert was working as an artist in France before he came to England, and painted the soldier miniature for a family there," he suggested.

I nodded. "Entirely possible. And then that family fell on hard times and had to sell some of their possessions, putting the miniature – eventually – into the hands of Lord Winstanley's agent."

"We could try to find out exactly when Rambert came to England," said Wilson.

"Perhaps," I said. "If we could identify the Englishman who first went to Mrs Anderson's with Rambert, he might know a little more."

We turned into Carburton Street, and coming towards us from the direction of Portland Road was Martha. My heart leapt a little as it always does on seeing her out and about, as though it can never quite believe that such a fine woman should be my wife. She was carrying a basket loaded with packages, and Wilson stepped forward smartly and took it from her. She smiled up at him.

"Thank you, William," she said, "and it is good that I catch you. I have just passed a woman selling mackerel, and as it is the end of the day she has let me have one extra. Will you join us? We can send a message to your mother."

"I am very fond of mackerel, Mrs Plank," said Wilson.

"That's settled, then," said my wife with satisfaction, and walked ahead of us up Norton Street. She would deny it if I suggested it, but I strongly suspected that she had bought the so-called extra fish on purpose, hoping to be able to feed our young constable again. Money was tight in the Wilson household, that we knew: with Wilson providing for a widowed mother, two almost grown sisters and three little ones while taking home only a junior constable's wage, rations were spread thin. The more suppers we fed him, the more was left for the others in that crowded attic on Brill Row.

After a fine fish apiece followed by a handsome wedge of bread pudding with apple, we two constables leaned back in our chairs and continued our discussion of the Winstanley miniature.

"I could call on Mrs Anderson tomorrow," offered Wilson, "and see what she can remember of Mr Rambert's English friend."

Martha paused as she cleared the table. "Have you considered the uniform?" she asked.

"The uniform?" I asked.

"The man in the miniature," replied Martha. "You said he was wearing a red military coat. If you can find out when that uniform was being worn, that will tell you when the portrait was painted."

I looked at Wilson.

"I know, I know," he said. "A quick-witted wife can be a benefit as well as a torment. You have told me many times."

Martha swiped at me with her cloth and I ducked.

CHAPTER FIVE

Markwick and the military

THURSDAY 11TH JANUARY 1827

"Well, that's no difficulty at all," said Thomas Neale.

Tom had been the office-keeper at Great Marlborough Street since its opening in 1793, when he was a young man of Wilson's age. Now he was about ten years my senior, but every time someone suggested he might fancy a quiet life at home, he rolled his eyes and reminded us about Mrs Neale. None of us had ever met this martinet, but Tom's tales of her demands and rages were frequently offered as an explanation for his fondness for his front counter at Great Marlborough Street, and when you consider the sorts he

31

saw across that very counter, I could only imagine the horror of Mrs Neale.

Wilson frowned slightly. "What do you mean, Mr Neale?"

"My sister's lad, young Archie, was taken on a couple of years ago as apprentice to a tailor in Conduit Street. A military tailor. If you can describe the uniform to him – if Sam here can remember enough about it – he can tell you what it might be. He's a bright boy is Archie, determined to do well, and he spends hours reading catalogues and almanacs – learning the trade, as he calls it. Here." Tom took a scrap of paper and wrote a note on it. "That's the address; ask for Archibald Markwick and tell him that his Uncle Tom sent you."

I pushed open the door of the tailor's shop. This was a far cry from the usual crammed and chaotic shops generally to be found in London. If a gentleman had not the inclination to summon a tailor to his own rooms, he might feel very comfortable coming to this elegant establishment. On either side of the shop were long wooden counters polished to a high shine, and lining the walls, up to the ceiling, were cabinets of drawers made of the same rich wood. A neat label was slipped into a metal frame on the front of each drawer, indicating the contents – gloves, handkerchiefs, cravats and the like. A single tailor's form – headless and armless, but with a fine military bearing in the face of these cruel losses – stood at the rear of the shop, sporting a dashing frock coat in deep blue. A heavy curtain hung across the back of the shop, leading – I guessed – to the workshop at the rear, and to stairs up to a dressing salon above where a gentleman would be measured and fitted. On hearing the shop door, the tailor appeared through this curtain.

As you would expect, he was dressed impeccably. That is not to say showily, but in refined taste – to demonstrate the skills of his workshop without putting the style of his customers to shame. His buckskin trousers were slim and fitted from thigh to ankle, and his coat, although plain of adornment, was in the latest cut, neat to the waist and wide, perhaps even slightly puffed, on the shoulders. His cravat was economical but sparkling white, and his waistcoat was a muted shade of blue. He ran a practised eye over the two of us.

"Constables. I hope that you are not here on a matter of your business rather than of mine," he said.

"We seek information, that is all," I said. I took out my notebook to prove it. "And you are Mr…?"

"Hunter," he said. "Josiah Hunter, tailor. As you can see." He indicated the shop with a flourish. "And you seek information about the latest fashions from Paris? The newest knot for a cravat?"

I shook my head. "We have been sent to see one of your apprentices. We are trying to identify a uniform that we have seen as part of our enquiry into a murder." The tailor's eyebrows shot up but he remained silent – I daresay discretion is an important characteristic for those who regularly see gentlemen in their underclothes. I continued. "Your apprentice's uncle says that the lad knows a great deal about military uniforms, that he makes something of a study of them."

Hunter smiled. "You will mean Markwick, I daresay." I nodded. "Come through, then, and let us put his knowledge to the test."

The tailor held aside the curtain for us, and Wilson and I walked through into the rear of the shop. A small vestibule came first, with, as I had expected, stairs leading upwards. Another curtain was ahead of us, and behind that was the workroom. A long, broad bench filled most of this room, with stools on either side, while shelves from floor to ceiling on both walls housed bolts of material, spools of thread, boxes of buttons, cards of braid and every other detail a gentleman might demand. In the corner was a stove with several irons warming on it. The back wall of the premises was made almost entirely of glass panes, to provide the light needed for the fine work demanded of these men.

"This is Mr Jackson, one of our senior cutters," said Hunter, tapping an elderly gentleman on the shoulder. This fellow stood upright, putting a hand to the small of his back, and peered at me short-sightedly. "He has been with us since His Majesty was in a skeleton suit, is that not right, Mr Jackson?" The old man wheezed by way of reply. "And this is our other senior cutter, Mr Jackson." Hunter indicated the other side of the table, and another elderly man hauled himself to his feet. He was identical to the first Mr Jackson. Wilson gaped.

The first Mr Jackson said nothing, but the second stretched his lips into something approaching a smile. "Aye," he said hoarsely. "Born together, live together, work together, and one day die together." From the lack of reaction from anyone else, I took it for an old joke.

"The only way to tell them apart," said Hunter, "is that Mr Jackson is much more talkative than Mr Jackson." He seemed to recall the purpose of our visit. "And where is young Markwick?"

By now both Jacksons were once more bent over their work, but the silent one raised an arm and pointed to the back door, and at that moment it opened to admit a lad of about fifteen buttoning his trousers. He stopped dead when he saw us all staring at him.

Hunter beckoned him in. "Ah, Markwick – you have visitors. These constables wish to have a word with you."

The colour drained from Markwick's face. "Is it my uncle? Is he unwell?"

"No, no, not at all," I said hurriedly. "We have a question about a uniform, and Tom – Mr Neale – suggested you. He sends his regards. Here: sit down and we will explain."

Hunter returned to the shop and the two Jacksons picked up their chalk once more. As Markwick pulled up a stool alongside me, I could see the family resemblance; I remembered Tom having fine, thick red hair like this when I first knew him.

"Now, Archie, I have seen a portrait – a miniature portrait – of a fellow in a military coat. Your uncle tells me that you have made a study of military uniforms. And I need to know what sort of coat it is, so that I can work out when and where the portrait was painted. Do you understand?" Markwick nodded. "The portrait shows the man from the waist up, but you can tell that it is a short coat. It is red, with black turned-back lapels down the front. Quite wide. The collar is likewise black, with silver embroidery on it. There are matching rows of gold buttons all down the front."

"A double row on each side, or a single?" asked Markwick.

I closed my eyes, the better to picture the miniature again in my mind. "Single," I said. "About ten plain gold buttons down each side. And the cuffs are black, again with silver embroidery. And there is silver embroidery around each buttonhole."

Markwick thought for a moment.

"We think it may be French," I suggested.

He shook his head emphatically. "Oh no, definitely not French. Blue and green are their colours. I think some of the hussars have a red pelisse – a short cape worn over one shoulder – but no red coats."

"So English, then?" asked Wilson, looking up from his notebook.

"Not with that silver embroidery, no," said Markwick. "You are sure of that detail?"

I nodded. "Leaves, I think," I said. "A trailing line of leaves around the cuff."

"In that case, I would hazard Italian."

"Italian?" Wilson and I said together.

"Or perhaps out of a dressing up box," said the young lad with a smile. Wilson and I looked at each other. Out of the mouths of babes.

"Not French at all, then," said Mr Conant.

I shook my head. "Young Markwick was not sure it was an Italian coat, but he was certain that it was not French."

"Hah!" said the magistrate. "So where does this leave poor old Winstanley and his boasts of having driven a hard bargain with those French widows?"

"Well, the miniature could still be French – that is, painted by a Frenchman – but of a foreign subject," I suggested.

This time Conant shook his head. "No: when I took the miniature back to him, Winstanley said that his dealer had told him that it was a portrait of the youngest son of the family – the French family – that had owned the entire collection. Spun him a sorry tale of a poor weeping mama forced to sell the family treasures – even tried to raise the price a little, apparently, when Winstanley showed sympathy for her misfortunes."

"So who is lying?" I asked. "The family selling their treasures, to get a better price? The agent, to feather his own nest more lavishly?" I swallowed, but it had to be said. "Or Lord Winstanley, to hide how he really acquired the collection?"

Conant smiled tightly. "I see your point, Sam, but Winstanley is a fool. He lacks the wit to conjure a plan like that, or the skill to carry it out." The magistrate walked across to one of the large windows overlooking the street and gazed out; after years of acquaintance with the man, I knew this meant that he was pondering a troubling idea. I waited. After two or three minutes, he turned back to me. "I think we need to learn more about this agent. I shall call again on Winstanley and ask for his name. I shall hint that I am interested in making some purchases of my own. Winstanley will not be able to resist lording it over me with his greater knowledge of the marketplace. Thank heavens for stupid men, constable, for their behaviour is as predictable as it is exasperating."

CHAPTER SIX

Modern travel

TUESDAY 16TH JANUARY 1827

"Now that is a smart uniform," said Martha, looking approvingly at the guard, who was overseeing the loading of the mail coach with an air of importance, his thumbs tucked into the pockets of his fine scarlet coat with its rich blue lapels, his black hat with the gold band proudly on his head. When we were courting I had often teased Martha about her fondness for a man in uniform – indeed, I knew that this was partly what had drawn me to her attention – and it seemed that little had changed.

"I hear they earn a handsome wage," said Wilson.

"Aye," I said, "but that is to keep them honest. The mail is in their sole charge from here until it is unloaded from the coach. It is a heavy responsibility, and the temptations are many. You see those long pockets of his?"

Wilson and Martha both looked at the guard and nodded. "Well, in those he carries a blunderbuss and two pistols, to warn off robbers and other trouble." Martha's hand tightened on my arm and I cursed myself for my tactlessness. I tried to distract her. "Look up there, on the roof of the coach, just in front of where the guard rides – it's his post horn. He blows on that, and the toll gates are opened to allow the coach to gallop through unstopped."

"I wish you were in your uniform, Sam, if there are to be robbers – they would hesitate to harm a constable," said Martha quietly.

"But I cannot meet this agent Mr Lagrange dressed as a constable, my love," I said. "As far as he is concerned, I am John Snaith, representing a young gentleman who has recently come into money and has an interest in acquiring French paintings for personal enjoyment."

Martha coloured slightly, and Wilson coughed. We moved to one side as porters made their way from the yard of the General Post Office and started piling up boxes and bags alongside the coach. There were five coaches lined up in the street, all destined for different routes. Like their guards, they too were finely decorated: the upper part of each coach was glossy black, while the doors and lower panels were maroon. The wheels were a bright red, and on each door was the royal coat of arms in gold, with "Royal Mail" written around it and the route above that – I had identified mine from the neatly-lettered "Dover – London". Standing ready in the traces, the four horses assigned to my coach pawed and blew out clouds of breath in the evening air, doubtless sensing the excitement and impatient to be gone. Mine was a superior vehicle, promising speed and – for those of us lucky enough to be booked inside, at least – some degree of comfort. I had been prepared for a more bracing ride outside, galloping through the night with the driver, but Mr Conant had insisted on the difference being paid; he was concerned that, should Mr Lagrange see me arrive in Sittingbourne, he must believe me to be in the employ of a wealthy man.

The drivers called out for passengers to board, and I turned to Martha. "I will be home before you know it," I said. "By breakfast time on Thursday. And ready for my bed, after two nights on the move." I kissed her on the cheek. "It is only Kent, my love – not Indochina," I said softly.

"I shall see Mrs Plank home, sir," said Wilson solemnly.

I climbed into the coach and took my seat, nodding a greeting to my fellow passengers – two other men. I had not seen them board, so I assumed they had met the coach earlier when it made a passenger stop at Piccadilly. I could have boarded then too, of course, but Martha had wanted to come and watch the mail depart, and it was certainly quite a spectacle. I tucked my small bag behind my legs and put my hat on my knees; every inch of space in the mail coach was used for bags and boxes, with passengers and their belongings very much an afterthought. The porter reached into the coach with one more canvas bag and shoved it under my seat – its label said "Calais", for of course much of the Dover mail was destined for packet boats and the Continent.

The guard poked his head in. "All ready, gentlemen?" he asked. We nodded, and he slammed the door shut, rattling it from the outside to check. I heard the creak as he climbed onto his platform at the rear of the coach. There were a few seconds of almost silence, and then the bells of St Clement's start to toll the hour. As they finished at eight o'clock precisely, the guard sounded his post horn and we pulled away. I looked out and saw Martha and Wilson standing arm in arm, each with a hand raised in farewell.

Modern travel may be fast, but it is far from comfortable. By the time I clambered down from the coach in Sittingbourne I was aching in every joint, and my head throbbed from the constant noise. The first few miles had been exhilarating as we bowled along, the guard blowing his horn with authority to warn all to give us right of way, but the speed of our passage meant that we had to work hard to hold ourselves upright and avoid being thrown against the side of the coach on every corner and bruised black and blue. All I had heard about the pride the mail drivers take in keeping to – or, if possible, beating – their timetable was true: as we approached each stop, the playing on the post horn became more frantic, to alert those waiting for us, and mail was all but thrown off the coach as we slowed, with new packages snatched up as we passed. When we were forced to come to a complete stop in order to change horses, we passengers were given only a minute to relieve ourselves, and warned that the coach would not wait for laggards. My three companions – a third had joined us in Dartford – were going all the way to Dover, and they looked at me almost enviously as I made my escape.

The Royal Victoria Hotel, although renamed after the princess and her mother stayed for the night a couple of years before my visit, had for a century been the Rose Inn, and its floral heritage was still obvious in the rose plaque high on the wall and the large rose sign hanging over the road. I walked into the grand entrance to the hotel, under a pillared canopy, and found the place as busy at half-past two in the morning – for that was the hour – as it would have been at midday. A young lad was standing behind a desk, checking off items on a list, and I went up to him.

"My name is Snaith," I said, "and I am here to meet a gentleman from France. His name is…"

"Lagrange," said a deep voice behind me. "Antoine Lagrange."

I turned around, and standing with his hand outstretched in greeting was Lord Winstanley's agent. He was about forty, I guessed, with wild, dark hair above a blunt face; his nose, which had been broken at least twice, had the high colour that testifies to a fondness for the bottle, and between his eyes was a deep furrow of mistrust. There was an unhealthy pallor to his skin, but then none of us looks at our best in the early hours.

"You are Sneth," he said with a heavy accent.

"John Snaith," I confirmed.

"Come, we will have some refreshment," said Lagrange, leading me into the parlour and through that into the snug. On his way he nodded at the innkeeper, who brought in a brimming tankard and a generous piece of pie for each of us, laid them on the table before the fire, and then pulled across the heavy curtain marking the doorway to the snug. We had it to ourselves, from which I gathered that Antoine Lagrange was well-known to the innkeeper.

The Frenchman took a deep drink from his tankard and then stabbed his pie with his fork, breaking off a large piece that he conveyed to his mouth, dropping crumbs down his front. With his other hand he brushed at his lapels.

"You like our English ale?" I asked.

He shrugged. "I am now familiar with it," he said. "I have been visiting your fine country for many years."

"But not London?" I asked.

"I am a paysan, Mr Sneth – a country boy. I do not like cities." He took another long drink and called out to the innkeeper. Within seconds a pot boy appeared with two more tankards – I would have to take care not to find myself jug-bitten.

"So you have never been to London?" I asked. He narrowed his eyes at me, and I scolded myself inwardly: I was acting like a constable, all questions. "I ask only because there are many gentlemen there, like my master, who would be glad of your services, I am sure."

Lagrange seemed satisfied. "Tell me about your master," he said, applying himself once more to the pie.

"The Honourable…" I held up a hand as though checking myself, "the gentleman whom I represent has recently come into his inheritance. A sizeable inheritance. He is still a young man, with few responsibilities beyond those of his class and connections, and, having recently had the good fortune to attend a showing of the collection of French miniatures owned by the father of a friend, he has expressed an interest in making a few acquisitions of similar works for himself."

Lagrange nodded as he dug around in a back tooth with his tongue. "This father of a friend – you talk of

Lord Winstanley?" he asked once he had excised whatever was troubling him.

"I do – but you must rest assured that Lord Winstanley himself has not given away your identity. His son was the one who passed your name to the gentleman with whom I am concerned."

"It is still a little too close for comfort, I think you say." I nodded. "But no matter. Your young gentleman – he is interested in military subjects, or the more…" he made a circle with his hand and I nodded again. "Ah, let us say the more classical compositions – the Muses at their toilette and the like, c'est ça?"

"And you know where such pieces can be found?" I asked, taking up my tankard so as not to arouse suspicion. A man who asks much and drinks little is unusual.

"I do." He glanced over at me and I raised my eyebrows questioningly. "You are aware, of course, Mr Sneth, of the turmoil in my country?" I nodded. "My family, like many others, was considered an enemy of the people, and my father took us into hiding – I was a child only. During the war I, well, I am a Frenchman, after all. But when I returned, my home, she was destroyed – and my family, all dead. All I have left of France is memories," he tapped the side of his head, "memories and an understanding of how the Frenchman thinks. The Lagrange name still counts for something, and I offer others in my position a way to survive their change in circumstances. You cannot eat a painting, I always remind them."

"And so you act as agent, finding buyers in England for these French treasures," I finished.

"Your countrymen have a fine appreciation for the talents of our French artists," said Lagrange. "And it is better to see their work cared for here than destroyed over there." He jerked his head in the general direction of the Channel and France.

"Indeed." I paused for a few moments as though considering a decision, and then continued. "When I return to London and tell my gentleman that I have found him an agent," at this, the Frenchman raised his tankard to me in salute, "how should we proceed?"

"You have already given me a good indication of the sort of collection we seek: small, intimate pieces, suited to the taste of a young single gentleman. When I find something suitable, I will send word to you in London – but not directly to you, of course." I cannot be certain, but I think Lagrange winked at me.

"Of course," I said.

"I will send a message care of Monsieur Pascal Renard. He is a banker; his house is near the Strand – Craven Street. Burnham and Renard."

CHAPTER SEVEN

Only a small vice

THURSDAY 18TH JANUARY 1827

"If you're this dusty," said Martha, standing in the yard and shaking my coat with her head turned away, "I can only imagine what it was like for the poor people sitting outside." She coughed and gave the coat another good shake.

I was splashing water over my face and chest, and reached out blindly for a cloth to dry myself. Spending nearly six hours sitting upright in a mail coach overnight was undoubtedly more comfortable than braving the cold and dust outside, but I still felt far from rested. I patted my face and went into the kitchen, shivering. Martha had put my clean shirt before the range to warm and I pulled it on gratefully, even though it now smelt slightly of sausages. I sat at the table and Martha came in, drying her hands.

"I've left your coat outside, to blow through," she said. "The buttons are dull, but I'll leave them until this evening." She took a plate from the cupboard and turned to the range to assemble my breakfast. "Did you eat as well as drink, with this Frenchman?"

Any married man knows that it is impossible to disguise the scent of ale on your breath, and Martha – daughter of a drunkard – has a particularly sensitive nose. She put the plate in front of me and I fell on it.

"After our talk," I said a couple of minutes later, "Lagrange left the hotel to meet the Dover stage – he had to return to France, he said. I had a bite to eat and then a walk around the town, but I found myself feeling drowsy. I asked the innkeeper where I could rest for the afternoon and he let me have use of a small back parlour, with a comfortable enough chair, and I settled in there with a newspaper. Good job I told the pot-boy of my plans, because by eleven in the evening I was fast asleep and would have missed the mail coach entirely. But he came in and woke me, and earned himself a handsome tip for doing so." I yawned widely. Martha stood and put her hand on her hips.

"Off with that shirt," she said. "You're going to bed for a couple of hours." I opened my mouth to object and then closed it again. Martha clapped her hands as though to catch the attention of a naughty child. "Shirt, Sam. I shall send word to Mr Neale not to expect you until later, and I'll wake you at noon."

By the time Martha followed me upstairs to pull the curtains I was in bed and all but asleep, although I felt her kiss on my forehead. Four hours later she came back upstairs and gently shook me awake.

"William is downstairs. I think he was worried about you," she said, smiling.

"Unlikely," I said, shrugging into the shirt that she handed me. "I daresay he wants to hear all about the mail coach and how fast it went."

Wilson was sitting at the table and looked up with a smile when I walked into the kitchen. In front of him was a cup of hot chocolate and a thick wedge of walnut loaf.

"Mrs Plank said you'd be up soon," he said, "and I thought you might have some news."

I sat down and Martha brought over a drink and slice of loaf for me. I had a bite and then told Wilson about my visit to Sittingbourne and the meeting with Lagrange. He listened carefully, making diligent notes in his book as I spoke. In between, he dabbed at the loaf crumbs on his plate with his finger. Martha wordlessly served him another slice. I remember being that age, able to eat anything without fear of becoming a puff guts. At the end of my tale, he shook his head wonderingly.

"Six hours!" he said. "Only six hours to travel, what, more than fifty miles, with three stops along the way. What a speed!"

I looked at Martha and winked at her while draining my cup. "And now I shall go to see this French banker, Renard," I said.

Wilson frowned slightly. "Is that wise, do you think, sir?" he asked.

"You think not?" I replied.

"As you tell it," said Wilson, looking back over his notes, "you do not expect to hear from the banker until the agent – Lagrange – sends word that he has found something." Wilson looked up at me. "If you go to see Mr Renard now, will he not think that you are too cautious – perhaps even suspicious?"

Martha folded her arms and looked at me, a little smile on her lips. I knew what she meant: Wilson was starting to think for himself.

"You may well be right," I said. Wilson flushed with pleasure. "But we cannot leave things to chance – we are not simply at the mercy of events, are we?"

"Indeed not, sir," said Wilson. "We can ready ourselves for when this banker does contact you."

"Always know more about a man than he knows about you," I said. Wilson nodded. "And how do you propose that we learn about this banker Renard without meeting him?"

Wilson thought for a moment. "Talk to someone who knows the world of banking," he said. Then he looked at me brightly. "Your friend, sir – Mr Freame."

Wilson and I had just turned the corner into Cheapside when the door of the banking house of Freame and Company opened and out came the man himself. I like to flatter myself that Edward Freame and I had become good friends in the two years of our acquaintance, and as he walked briskly down the steps of his bank and caught sight of me, a genuine smile appeared on his face.

"Constable Plank," he said warmly, holding out his hand to shake mine. "And this tall fellow must be Constable Wilson, of whom you have told me so much." He grasped Wilson's big hand in his two neat ones, and beamed up at him. "It is a great pleasure to see you both, but as ever..." he dragged his watch out of his pocket and looked at it, "I am late. As ever. My wife despairs, my clerk chastises, and yet..." He shrugged. "It is only a small vice, I comfort myself."

"So you are on your way to an appointment," I said. "That is a shame, as we were hoping to have a word with you."

"To reach my appointment I need only my legs – my ears are yours," said the banker. "Come: we shall walk together." He set off eastwards along Cheapside, tipping his hat at almost everyone we passed. "Bankers to a man," he said with a wry smile. "We are thick on the ground hereabouts."

"It is a banker we wanted to ask you about," I said. "A French banker. Pascal Renard." I looked at Freame but he made no reaction, good or bad.

"Renard, Renard," he repeated. "Ah yes: Burnham and Renard. But you will not find Mr Renard in this part of town, constable. His house is off the Strand, I believe."

"Craven Street," I confirmed.

"And indeed, you will not find Mr Burnham in London at all." Freame stopped to let a carriage roll past and tipped his hat at its occupant before proceeding into Poultry.

"And why is that?" I asked. Just then the bell of St Mildred tolled the hour.

"Ah, and so you see – late again," said Freame, half to himself. "But," he stopped in his tracks and Wilson had to use some fancy footwork to avoid cannoning into him, "a reputation for tardiness has its uses. The gentleman I am meeting knows me of old, and expects me to be at least five minutes late. He and I are meeting just there," Freame pointed to a coffee house over the road, "at three, and so he expects me at five past. Which gives us about four minutes, gentlemen." He smiled encouragingly.

"Mr Burnham," I prompted.

"Ah yes, Mr Burnham. As I understand it, Mr Burnham is a country gentleman, busy with his animals and fields in, well, Norfolk, I believe." Freame waved his arm in the general direction of the north, in the dismissive manner of the Londoner who cannot understand why a man would choose to live anywhere but in the metropolis. "As a consequence he knows a great deal about animals and fields and very little about banking. He is what we call a sleeping partner: he provides money, but has no other involvement."

Wilson looked up from his notebook. "And why..." he started.

"Why would Mr Renard need such a partner?" said Freame. "For many, it is the money, of course – but not in this case. Mr Renard comes from a French family of note, and therein lies his problem: his name. Our tastes are changing, thank goodness, but we English are still a little wary of our French neighbours. And so Mr Renard seeks to reassure his clients by attaching to his own name that of a respectable and trustworthy English family: the Burnhams."

"And Mr Renard – is he also respectable and trustworthy?" I asked.

"Fox by name, you mean?" asked Freame with a smile. I nodded. "To be honest, I have had little to do with the man, professionally or personally. But I can ask those who know him better, if you like. Discreetly, of course;

we bankers are well schooled in the art of discretion. And now my five minutes of latitude are expiring and I risk being rude, so I must leave you." The banker touched his hat in farewell. As he crossed the road he looked back over his shoulder. "I shall send word if my enquiries bear fruit."

CHAPTER EIGHT

A first step to French

FRIDAY 19TH JANUARY 1827

As I leaned against the wall with one hand, stamping the mud from my boots, I realised how much I missed coming home to the comforting sounds of Martha going about her business – the clatter of pots, the sizzle of the iron, the gentle humming of a half-heard tune. As the wife of a constable, Martha has grown used to unpredictability and interruptions. She has perfected the art of keeping a meal (and a bed) warm to await my return when I am summoned to duty, and she only rarely complains when our plans are thrown into disarray by my work. But now, on at least two evenings a week, I would arrive home before her and have to light the lamps myself and put the dinner to heat.

I did not object to the tasks; it was simply that returning to an empty dwelling was a sensation I had been glad to leave behind with bachelorhood all those years ago.

It was cold comfort to remind myself that the change was thanks in no small part to my own boasting. Last year, after I had sung Martha's praises to him once too often, Edward Freame had asked to meet her and, in that gentle, smiling way of his, had persuaded her to join him in a new venture. He and his fellow Quakers were keen to improve the lot of young girls, whose education is so often overlooked in favour of that of their brothers, and in consequence had founded a number of girls' schools. One of these is specifically for girls who have had an unfortunate – let us be honest, an immoral – start in life, and Freame wanted to augment their studies of the basics of reading and writing with a consideration of what he (and now Martha and I) called 'the ways of the world'. And knowing that Martha – the wife of a constable and herself brought up in far from coddled circumstances – had a more realistic view of things than many women, he asked her to assist with the instruction of these girls.

Martha was initially reluctant; her own lack of education is a cause of some shame for her, despite my best efforts to convince her that we should feel shame only for those decisions over which we exercise control. How could she go against the orders – and fists – of her drunken father? But with my encouragement and

Freame's confidence that she would be the perfect instructress, she took to it like a duck to water, and so I found myself sharing my wife's attention for the first time in years.

I was changing out of my work shirt when I heard the back door open and Martha called up to me. When I went down to the kitchen, she was tying on her apron. I kissed the cheek that she turned to me and sat down, waiting to hear about her day at the school. On the table was a small book and I picked it up. It was a very little volume, barely bigger than my hand, with a plain buff cover and a simple border. "A New Pronouncing French Primer; Or First Step to the French Language" was the title, and the author was the impressive-sounding Gabriel Suranne, French Master to the Scottish Military and Naval Academy.

Martha looked over her shoulder at me. "The girls are starting French lessons," she explained, "to improve their memorisation and their reading, and I borrowed this so that I can keep up with them. I thought you might like it too, now that you are keeping company with French artists and French bankers."

"Who all speak English," I said, "as indeed they should, here in England." But I opened the little book and started to read. "They're certainly a God-fearing lot, the French," I said. "The very first word they give you is 'Dieu'."

"I know that one already – God," said Martha.

"Prayer, priest, sin, confession," I continued. "A bit keen on the immortal soul, your Frenchie." I turned over a few more pages. "Ah, here's something a little more down to earth. 'J'ai des bas en soie'."

Martha turned around. "That sounds pretty. What does it mean?"

"I have silk stockings," I said, winking at her. She pouted at me. "And here's what you should say to me in reply: 'Sans adieu, à ce soir'. I shall see you again tonight." I put down the book and caught hold of my wife as she leaned across me to put a dish on the table, pulling her onto my lap. "You were right, Mar – French is a language well worth learning."

CHAPTER NINE

Fox by name

WEDNESDAY 24TH JANUARY 1827

It was almost a week since we had visited Edward Freame and, having heard nothing from him about the French banker, I decided that I would call on Renard myself and ask him about the agent Lagrange. I would meet him as Constable Sam Plank; there was no need to introduce him to John Snaith.

A bitter January wind whistled up from the river as Wilson and I turned into Craven Street.

"An unusual place for a banking house, is it not?" asked Wilson, looking about him at the prosperous terraces of tall buildings that flanked the street, their ground floors fronted in white stone and the upper storeys made of neat, dark brick. I was pleased to see him taking close notice and learning to read his surroundings.

"Indeed," I agreed, "but as more people of substance move to this part of London, they will become less inclined to journey all the way into the city to discuss their affairs. This street is already home to several lawyers, and just around the corner we have Whitehall and all that that entails."

We reached the door of number 37, with its discreet brass plaque admitting it to be the premises of Burnham and Renard. Wilson knocked and we waited on the colourful tiled step. A minute later the door was opened and we were beckoned in by perhaps the oldest banking clerk I had seen in my life; the man was eighty if he was a day. The undersides of his coat sleeves were shiny where he leaned on his desk all day and the ink stains on the fingers of his right hand would never disappear, but after taking our hats and pointing us towards two chairs once we had asked to see the banker, he trotted into the back rooms of the bank with great energy, and then returned to hop onto his stool with surprising agility, pushing his pince-nez back onto his nose before picking up his pen and returning to his ledger. Wilson and I raised our eyebrows at each other.

After about five minutes we heard a door open and out came Mr Renard. Perhaps I was too influenced by my spruce friend Freame, but I was taken aback to see that the Frenchman was tall, broad, generous of girth, extravagantly bearded, untidy in his dress – in short, not at all what I had expected. What the two men had in common was the warmth of their welcome.

"Gentlemen," said the banker, holding out his hand. "My clerk tells me that I am being visited by two constables – should I be worried?" His smile suggested that very little would worry him, and he pumped my hand vigorously. Wilson very rarely has to look up to another man, but this was one such occasion.

"Monsieur Renard," I began.

The banker clasped his hands in front of him. "Constable," he said, "I thank you for the courtesy, but I think we will all be more comfortable – your lips, my ears – if we stick with English. I have been in this fine country for many years now, and I am Mister Renard. I have the brush to prove it, even if I do still sound a little foreign." He pointed to his fine beard, which did indeed have a reddish tinge to it.

I smiled. "Mr Renard, we would like to talk to you about one of your clients. An art dealer called Antoine Lagrange." I watched Renard carefully as I said this name, and although he mastered it quickly, I swear I saw a hardening of his features.

"In that case, gentlemen, I fear you are on a fool's errand. Lagrange is no client of this bank – I know him in a personal capacity only."

"And in that case, Mr Renard, we are even more keen to speak to you about him," I said firmly.

The banker looked at me and shrugged. "Very well – but as this is not a banking matter, we shall discuss it elsewhere." He glanced at the clock on the wall. "I find my thoughts turning to food," he patted his stomach, "and my daughter will be preparing a meal upstairs. Come: you shall join me."

Wilson and I followed Renard into the back of the bank and up a narrow flight of stairs to the apartment above. As he had predicted, the dining table was already laid with several covered dishes, two places set with plates and forks.

"Sylvie," the banker called, "we are two more to dine. Plates, if you please." He indicated that we should sit. "My wife, sadly, is no longer with us, but I am blessed with a daughter and she cares for her old papa."

As if on cue the door opened and in came Sylvie Renard, carrying another large covered dish, her dress shielded by a plain apron and her hair caught up in a bonnet to protect it from the steam in the kitchen. Wilson and I rose to our feet. The young woman put the dish on the table and curtseyed to us, her eyes flashing at her father.

"Please forgive my appearance, gentlemen," she said. "My father gave me no indication that we were expecting company." She put a self-conscious hand to her hair. "Do help yourselves." She left the dining room.

The banker leaned forward and moved the large dish into the centre of the table. He caught me looking at it and smiled.

"Amusing, no?" he said, indicating the lid of the large dish, which had the usual fancy designs – countryside scenes in pink curling borders – but was topped with a handle in the shape of a small dog scratching its ear. "From a factory in Marseille run by la Veuve Perrin – the Widow Perrin, as you would call her. My wife liked to collect it, as you can see." He took the lids off all the dishes and smelt each one in turn, giving little grunts of approval. "Here," he said, ladling food onto our plates, "you will like this one – from our homeland – and this too, this you will enjoy..." He paused, a full spoon hovering over Wilson's plate. "Constable?" he said. Renard looked at me and I looked at Wilson. He stood absolutely motionless, gazing at the door to the kitchen. The banker caught my eye and winked. "She is strong-minded, you know," he said, "and with that red hair – phew! Quite a temper. Like her late mother." Wilson blinked rapidly and sat down.

The door opened again and Miss Renard returned, without her apron or bonnet. Her hair, a rich red indeed, was caught in a hasty bun at the back of her neck, with one long curl escaping to hang over her shoulder. I had some sympathy for Wilson; I too have a weakness for women with unruly curls. Wilson leapt to his feet again, and Miss Renard inclined her head in acknowledgement and then sat between her father and me.

The banker controlled his amusement with some difficulty. "These two gentlemen are constables, my dear – Constable Plank, and Constable Wilson." He indicated each of us with his fork. "They have come to talk to me about Antoine. Mr Lagrange."

"Indeed, Papa," said the young lady. "Although it is some months, surely, since we heard from him." She took a piece of bread and dipped it into the food on her plate. "Tell me, Constable Plank, just what is it that a constable does?"

"A constable, miss," I said, "works for a magistrate. If the magistrate is told that a crime has been committed and wishes to speak to someone about it – the suspect, perhaps, or a witness – he sends out a constable to find that person and bring them to him. Constable Wilson and I work for the magistrates in Great Marlborough Street – in Piccadilly."

"And your magistrates wish to speak to Mr Lagrange?" she asked.

I paused; I had no wish to lie to Miss Renard, but nor could I tell her the truth. Her father sensed my hesitation, and perhaps also my unease.

"It is not for us to question the constables, my dear – it is their job to question us," he said gently. "And now," he continued quickly as his daughter opened her mouth again to speak, "we will all enjoy our meal."

"Bon appétit," I said.

"Hah!" said the banker delightedly. "I see that you speak French, monsieur."

I shook my head. "Far from it, sir, far from it. But my wife – Mrs Plank – works at an educational establishment for young girls who have been rescued from unfortunate circumstances. They are of course instructed in the skills that will serve them well – cooking, sewing and the like – but those who fund the school wish them also to learn some finer things. And the latest idea of the senior mistress is that a few words of French might stretch their minds and encourage them."

The banker nodded. "A laudable aim, monsieur. A woman who knows more than her stove and her needle makes a much more amusing and worthwhile wife, is that not so, Constable Wilson?" And he winked at Wilson, who flushed a deep red and could only nod.

Miss Renard leaned towards her father. "Papa," I heard her say, "j'ai une idée."

Her father listened, chewing all the while, and then waved his fork towards me and said, "Well, you should suggest it to the constable."

Miss Renard smiled prettily at me. "Constable Plank, I am interested to hear about this educational establishment, and would like to help. I am no teacher, of course, and my papa needs me here to care for him, but perhaps I could attend once a week to talk to the girls in French. They would be able to practise, and would also hear the correct accent." She said this last word in the French way, to illustrate her point – up until then, there had been nothing in her speech to give away that she was anything but English.

"A very kind offer, miss," I said, "and I shall mention it to Mrs Plank this very evening."

After we had eaten, Miss Renard cleared the table and, at a signal from her father, went into the kitchen, leaving the three of us. Wilson stared at the kitchen door for a minute before gathering himself and taking out his notebook.

"Mr Renard," I began, "could you tell me how you know Antoine Lagrange?"

"I have known Lagrange for perhaps eight years," said the banker. "Yes: we met when my dear wife was still with us." He stopped and Wilson and I waited. One of the hardest lessons for a young constable – indeed, for any young man – to learn is that of patience, but if you rush in before other people, you lose the chance to see what they would have done in your place. So we said nothing. After a long pause, Renard spoke again. "We discovered that we shared an interest in art, Antoine and I. Paintings in particular. French paintings." He waved his arm to indicate the walls of his dining room, on which were hung several indifferent pictures of countryside scenes – people at the harvest, a man leading a horse and cart and the like. "Mementoes."

"Do you miss France?" I asked.

"The France of today is not the country I left, constable," said the banker, "but surely every man hopes to be buried in the land of his birth." I raised an eyebrow. "Although not soon, of course," added Renard with a bark of laughter. He slapped his chest with his palm. "I am in good health, thank the Lord."

"Indeed," I said. "And your shared interest in art, with Mr Lagrange. Was that the extent of it – an interest – or did it go further than that? Into a business, perhaps?" I could feel rather than see Wilson pause in his writing to look up at the banker: faces can often tell more than words.

"Business is far too formal a word for our arrangement, constable," said the banker. "It was more of an agreement – an understanding."

"And what did you understand by it, Mr Renard?"

"I have a number of wealthy clients, constable. And such men like to spend their money on items that are pleasing to the eye. Paintings from France are very popular: by owning them, the Frenchman shows his patriotism and the Englishman his education." The banker smiled. "Sometimes a client will mention to me that he wishes to make such a purchase, and I will pass on his wish to Lagrange."

"Who can make their wishes come true," I concluded.

"Exactly, constable."

"And yet you said that Mr Lagrange is not himself one of your clients?" I asked.

Renard shook his head. "Sadly, no. I have yet to persuade Antoine of the benefits of entrusting his money to a banker."

I smiled, and looked over at Wilson. "I think we have all we need for now, Mr Renard." I stood. "Thank you for your hospitality, and please do thank your daughter for the delicious meal. And I am sure Mrs Plank will be delighted to hear of Miss Renard's generous offer of assistance with French conversation practice for her girls."

The banker led us downstairs and through the small banking hall. The ancient clerk looked up at us, nodded in farewell and bent his head again to his ledger.

As if reading my mind, Renard said quietly to me, "Greenwood has been with me for many, many years, constable. He should perhaps retire to his fireside, yes, but he is a widower and prefers to have our company during the day. He has had much sadness in his life – a beloved grandson killed at Toulouse – and his work is still good, so Sylvie and I, we watch over him."

I thought of Henri Causon, whose son had died at Leipzig – so many years of war, so many lost young men.

We reached the front door of the banking house and Renard held it open for us. As Wilson and I stepped out into the street, I turned to ask the banker one last question.

"Mr Renard, have you ever heard Mr Lagrange mention an artist called Rambert – Louis Rambert?"

"A Frenchman?" asked Renard. I nodded. "I knew a Rambert once, as a schoolboy, but he was François Rambert. Thank you for your visit, constables." And he stepped back inside the bank and closed the door.

I looked at Wilson.

"But sir," he said, "he did not answer the question."

"And that gives us the answer we need," I replied.

Although he was generally content to leave me to follow my own nose, the magistrate John Conant liked me to make regular reports to him – not least so that he could explain to his fellow magistrates at Great Marlborough Street why I was not always waiting in the police office to execute any warrants that they might issue. With four other constables at their disposal my absences with Wilson were rarely an inconvenience, but there were occasional accusations of favouritism, or talk of my being Conant's personal constable. It was nonsense of course although, to be honest, both he and I would have welcomed such an arrangement were it possible, so matched were we in our interests.

I passed Conant's footman Thin Billy on the stairs up to the magistrate's dining room.

"Miss Lily is with him," he said as he skirted round me with a tray.

All of us who worked at Great Marlborough Street had grown to welcome the frequent visits of Conant's daughter Lily, not only for her own sake but for the good humour she invariably induced in her father, and indeed I heard her laughter as I knocked on the door.

"Constable Plank," she said with a smile as I walked in. "You have come to talk to my father – is your report too shocking for my maidenly ears?"

"Not at all, Miss Conant," I said.

"In that case, Lily, you may stay," said Conant, "as long as you pour the coffee and do not interrupt."

Once we were all settled, Lily sitting on a low stool beside her father as she had done since she was a little girl, I told the magistrate of my visit to the banker Renard. He listened carefully, nodding occasionally.

"So you think that he did know Rambert?" he asked once I had finished.

"The poor Frenchman who was killed?" asked Lily, disobeying her father's instruction to stay silent.

"The miniature painter, yes," I said.

"I wonder that there are any artists left in France," said Lily, "with so many of them here in London."

Her father and I looked at her. "So many of them?" asked Conant. "What do you mean, my dear?"

"Well, there's Rambert, and of course Monsieur Bonneville." She looked up at her father. "My art tutor. You remember, papa: my Thursday lessons at the gallery."

CHAPTER TEN

The copying of Lazarus

THURSDAY 25TH JANUARY 1827

The next day I met Miss Conant outside the gallery at eleven in the morning. From the outside it looked no different to the other grand houses in Pall Mall, with its three storeys, neat brickwork and fine large windows. But two years earlier the government had bought the art collection of the late Russian banker John Julius Angerstein from his estate, and this collection was now on display here, in his former home. A doorman let us in, tipping his hat as he recognised Lily.

"Mr Bonneville's ladies are already here, miss – the usual place," he said, nodding towards a grand doorway.

Lily led me through into a large room with high ceilings and wonderfully ornate plasterwork high on the walls, with swags and leaves and garlands both above and below the picture rail. And that picture rail certainly earned its living, as every patch of wall was covered with paintings of all sizes, from small individual portraits tucked in between larger works, to a huge Biblical scene, twice the height of a man. It was in front of this painting that Lily's classmates had gathered, their easels set up before them, and I handed Lily her folding easel and stool so that she could take her place among them. She shook off her coat and replaced it with a plain pinafore, to protect her dress from paint. She opened her beautiful wooden paintbox ("A present from my father," she had explained as she sat with it on her lap in the carriage, stroking its gleaming lid, "from Ackermann's – in the Strand") and took from her bag a roll of paper; unfurling it, she revealed a half-finished painting and, smoothing it down with her hands, she clipped it to her easel. Glancing around at the other easels, I placed Lily squarely in the middle of this company: more talented than some, but lagging behind others.

We had arrived just in time. I heard the street door open again, and moments later into the gallery swept a man who could only have been an artist. As he took off his hat with a flourish, while making an exaggerated bow to the assembled ladies, he revealed a bald pate, but around the sides his white hair remained thick and stood out around his head like a halo. The occasional glimpse that I caught of his trousers told me that they were pale buckskin, disappearing into fine shoes that would have been more suited to the ballroom than to the winter streets. As for a shirt or cravat I could see nothing, as over everything he wore a full-length, dark red, velvet coat with deep black lapels and cuffs which almost covered his hands; the coat was fastened at his throat with an ornate brooch such as a dowager might choose. I glanced at Lily and she quickly looked away, biting her lip.

"Bonjour to you all, mademoiselles," said Bonneville, looking at the group. His gaze held mine for moment, and then he continued. "Today we continue, do we not, with our study of this magnifique work of del Piombo," he turned and indicated with a wide sweep of his arms the enormous painting that had caught my eye, "showing the raising of Lazarus. Note, if you please," and here he moved closer to the painting and pointed towards it with an elegant cane, "the hands. Everywhere there are hands – pointing here, clutching there. Our Lord himself – see how one hands points at the poor Lazarus, and the other is raised to heaven. Hands, mademoiselles," he turned back to his audience, "they are difficult to draw. But this does not mean that we should not try. And if you struggle, remember that you have two models yourselves – just at the end of the arms." He smiled. "And so – begin, if you please."

Lily, along with every other lady in the group, bent her head to her easel. Bonneville made a slow circuit of the class, looking over each shoulder in turn, making a noise of encouragement or a comment at each easel. Once he had seen everyone, he came over to me.

"Monsieur, I have not seen you accompany Miss Conant before. You are..." He waited for me to complete the sentence.

"A family friend," I said.

He put his head a little to one side. "I see. A family friend. Such an attractive young lady is sure to attract the attention of many such – family friends."

I chose not to correct him; indeed, his misapprehension about the purpose for my visit could work to my advantage. People are usually more open about their own moral shortcomings if they feel themselves in similarly compromised company. And so I simply smiled.

"You are a connoisseur of art, sir?" asked the Frenchman, pronouncing the word with ease.

I shook my head. "I am not, no. I can appreciate the skill needed to create such works, especially when I witness the efforts of others to mimic them, but I will confess that my tastes lie... elsewhere."

Bonneville looked at me, his eyes appraising me sharply. "Sculpture?" he asked.

"Oh no," I said. "I like paintings, just not paintings like this." I indicated the crowded walls. "These are too... well-behaved." I continued more softly. "I prefer to admire the natural form."

"Miss Woodbridge," said Bonneville loudly, "I can see from here that you are scrubbing at your paper. You will make a big smear, no, and where on the canvas can you see a big smear by del Piombo? Nowhere, that is where." The young lady he had castigated quickly dropped her hand from her easel, while everyone else in the group bent more determinedly over their work. "Many gentlemen share your taste, sir," he continued to me in an undertone, "and I find myself in the fortunate position of being able to, shall we say, satisfy that taste. Come." He jerked his head towards the doorway and we retreated from the group. He reached into a deep pocket of his velvet coat and pulled out a small canvas bag with a drawstring. He opened it. "Hold out your hand," he said. I did so, and into it he tipped a miniature painting. I turned it to the light.

The painting was slightly smaller than my palm, with a plain gold frame. The image was of a young woman stepping out of her bath, a robe draped around her but artfully positioned so as to reveal her thighs and one breast. Her maid was helping her dry, lifting her mistress's arm, but as she did so she turned to see the door slightly ajar and a man peeping in at them. Was the maid encouraging the man to spy on her mistress, or warning her about him?

Bonneville was at my elbow, looking at the painting. "We men like to watch," he said, "and fortuitously, women like to be watched."

I turned the miniature over, and on the back was a tiny pair of initials – LR.

Lily glanced over her shoulder to see where I was.

"Very pretty," I said, handing the miniature back to the Frenchman, who slipped it back into its bag and then into his pocket.

"Painted by one of our very finest French miniaturists, and brought across the Channel three days ago. I am delivering it this very afternoon to the gentleman who commissioned it. I expect him to be pleased." He looked at me.

"So something similar could be..." I left the sentence unfinished, but Bonneville patted his pocket to show that he had understood.

"Should you wish something for your own collection, sir, you know how to find me," he said. And the Frenchman bowed and walked back to his class.

"I should warn Mr Conant," I said. "He will want to stop Lily attending."

Martha turned from the stove. "And if he does, the art teacher will realise that something is wrong." She sat down, drying her hands on her apron. "Do you think that Lily is in any danger from this man?" I frowned. "Does he seduce the young ladies?" She paused. "Does he ask them to pose for him?"

I shook my head. "I saw no sign of that. The pieces are painted in France, so I suppose the ladies in them are French."

Martha smiled. "Not that you had a good look, of course."

"The merest of glances – if that," I replied, straight-faced. "As for Bonneville, he appeared to be a good teacher; after our conversation, he went to each student in turn to check her progress, and Lily was full of praise for him on the way home. And we both know that our Miss Lily is not easy to please."

Martha leaned back. "In that case, Sam, I think that alarming Mr Conant would be unwise. Men rarely think clearly where their own daughters are concerned." I opened my mouth to protest but my wife held up her hand to stop me. "You are like a bandog when anyone sniffs around Alice, and she's not even your daughter." She smiled at me. "And we are both very glad to have such a fierce protector for her."

CHAPTER ELEVEN

The nature of art

FRIDAY 26TH JANUARY 1827

If I believed in such things, I would say that New-gate gaol was overseen by a malign spirit. More often than not when I walked past its forbidding walls, the skies would darken where until that moment they had been cloudless, and I would have to hurry to avoid a soaking. This morning exactly that happened, and I had just reached the end of Skinner Street when I saw a familiar figure hastening towards me from the other direction; with his wooden leg, John Wontner had such a distinctive gait that it was easy to recognise him – although his peg-leg did not slow him down one jot. We met at the corner of Newgate.

"Sam," he said genially, "are you come to see me?"

I shook my head. "I was on my way to the Fleet, to speak to a prisoner there."

There was a crack of thunder overhead.

"If you wish to shelter a while, you are welcome," he said, looking up at the sky, and I had to trot to keep up with him. He rapped loudly on the stout wooden door of the prison. A turnkey peered round it and then opened it wide, touching his cap, when he saw Wontner.

"Come in, come in, sir, and you too, constable, before the heavens open," he growled. My work took me so frequently to this ghastly place that my face was known to all who worked there – and to many who lived there.

Wontner and I walked to his office; I settled into the chair he kept for visitors while he hung up his coat and attempted, unsuccessfully, to clear a space on his desk for the bundle of papers he had brought in with him. In the end, he simply put them on top of an already tottering pile.

"Drink?" he asked. I nodded, and he poured two tumblers of barley water from the jug on his window-sill. Sons of topers either follow their fathers into the taverns or swear off liquor for life, and Wontner was of the latter persuasion. I glanced at the wall of his office, near the door, where a group of four portraits was hanging. I had noticed them before but never looked at them properly. Wontner followed my gaze.

"My wife's family: her sister and three brothers," he said. "Grace – my wife – painted them herself, some years ago now. I find them rather fine."

I stood and went to look at them. Each about the size of a man's hand, they were accomplished little portraits, although of course I could not comment on their accuracy. The eldest brother was shown with a book in his hand, the middle one holding a riding crop, and the youngest standing next to a skinny dog that looked up at him with adoration. The sister had a piece of embroidery idle in her lap, and looked directly out of the frame at the artist. There was a strong family resemblance in evidence: they all had thick brown hair and what might charitably be called a strong nose.

As though he could hear my thoughts, Wontner said, "Grace is the pretty one, I am pleased to say. The nose passed her by."

I turned and smiled at him. "I have been looking at plenty of portraits recently," I said.

"Indeed?" Wontner topped up his own tumbler and waved the jug at me.

"It began with the murder – we believe it to be murder – about three weeks ago of a French miniaturist called Louis Rambert," I said. I outlined what we had discovered so far. "And now I find myself thinking about the nature of art." Wontner raised an amused eyebrow. "Oh, I don't mean anything grandly philosophical," I said, "but it seems to me that when it comes to paintings, a copy is just as acceptable as the real thing. The art tutor Bonneville's class is evidence of that: perfectly lovely young ladies from perfectly respectable families are encouraged to sit in front of works of art and copy them. If someone does that with a coin, we send them to the gallows."

"Or with a share certificate," added Wontner. We fell silent for a moment as we thought of the banker Henry Fauntleroy, in whose case we had both been so closely involved.

"Miss Conant tells me that galleries will even exhibit works that are known to be copies, labelling them as 'after the school of'," I continued. "Sometimes it is impossible to tell whether a painting is by the artist who has signed it, or by one of his pupils – and apparently collectors are not concerned: the master's signature is proof that the work meets his standards of quality, no matter who actually painted it." I shook my head.

"But perhaps that is right," said Wontner. "A painting is for pleasure, after all, so what does it matter who created it?"

"Except if you deceive people," I replied. "If you tell them it is by one artist – and you charge them accordingly – and it is in fact by another." I stopped, because the keeper had leaned forward in his seat and was searching through the papers on his chaotic desk. There must have been some order in the chaos, however, as only moments later he held up a folder triumphantly.

"Here, Sam," he said. "If you are minded to ponder the nature of copies and forgeries, you might enjoy this." He opened the folder and read aloud from the paper on the top. "Thomas Sinclair, accused of falsely making, forging and counterfeiting the last will of James Robinson, merchant, deceased." He looked up at me. "The trial is on Monday morning, if you'd care to go." He jerked his head towards the door. "Old Bailey."

CHAPTER TWELVE

The ungrateful brother

MONDAY 29TH JANUARY 1827 – MORNING

As usual, the court at the Old Bailey reminded me of nothing so much as a bear pit. Although the ceilings were high and tall windows behind the bench provided plenty of light, the many steps and boxes and wooden screens which were used to divide the courtroom into its constituent parts for all the players – judges, jury, accused and so on – always made me feel hemmed in. Wilson and I found ourselves seats near the back of the court, away from the constant movement but with a good view of proceedings, and watched as prisoners were brought in to face trial.

The first we saw, a wretched servant girl accused of stealing three teaspoons from her master, was sentenced

to transportation for seven years and, from her lack of reaction, understood nothing of what was said. Next came
a more seasoned criminal, a rough-looking fellow of
about forty; he was found guilty of burglary and sentenced to death. The old woman who cried out at the
verdict – his mother, I guessed – would almost certainly
be the only one to mourn his passing. The third to appear
was our man, Thomas Sinclair. He was older than I had
expected, perhaps as much as seventy. He walked into the
courtroom leaning on a stick, and paused at the foot of
the steps to the dock before hauling himself up them.

"This one?" said Wilson in surprise. I nodded.

On the bench, beneath the gilded sword of justice sus-
pended on the crimson wall, sat the judge, Sir John Bay-
ley. His intelligent eyes missed little, I knew, and he too
looked taken aback at the age of the accused, shuffling
through his papers to check the details. He nodded at the
clerk.

This dreary fellow stood and intoned in a bored voice,
reading from the sheet of paper in his hand. "Thomas
Sinclair, you stand indicted for that, on the tenth of De-
cember last, you feloniously did falsely make, forge and
counterfeit a certain last will, purporting to be the will of
James Robinson, of Marylebone, merchant, deceased,
which said will is as follows: 'The whole of my property I
wish to give to my mother-in-law, if she survives me, my
brother having bad conduct – although I hope she will be

good to him, when she finds it necessary. James Robinson.'." The clerk looked up at the old man in the dock, then down again at the paper. "You also stand indicted for that you did utter and publish the same as true, knowing it to be false and counterfeit." The clerk put the paper down on the table and picked up his pen before turning again to the accused. "Thomas Sinclair, how say you? Are you guilty or not guilty of the said felonies?"

We all looked at the man in the dock. For his part, he drew himself as upright as he could, and said clearly, "Not guilty."

The clerk made a note of his response, and then asked him, "How will you be tried?"

Again, the response was spoken without faltering. "By God and my country."

I leaned towards Wilson. "I'm inclined to believe him," I said.

"Because he spoke so certainly?" asked Wilson.

I shook my head. "Because he stood so proudly as he said it. When a man stands so, he is proud of what he is saying and is filled with its truth."

The usual niceties completed – everyone sworn in and identified – the first to speak on behalf of Sinclair was Albert Kirby, a man of about the same age as the accused.

He was obviously nervous, but nonetheless spoke clearly and with conviction.

"I am perfectly acquainted with the prisoner," he confirmed. "He lived some years in my service." In answer to another question from the lawyer, he continued, "I have known him intimately since 1810, and less well for some years before that. In 1810 he came into my service as manager of my glass works in Southwark, and remained until 1816. He was principal manager and very important interests were entrusted to him. In that position he might have defrauded me of thousands of pounds without being detected, but he never defrauded me of a penny, and behaved always exceeding well and with fidelity. He left in August 1816 and commenced business on his own account, as agent for the sale of glass." The lawyer asked about money, and Kirby continued. "While he was in my service I gave him a hundred and fifty pounds a years, house rent, and coals – he had a wife and two children. If there was any change in his mode of living after he left me, it was for the worse – there was certainly no improvement."

Wilson made a note in his book. "Which means," he whispered to me, "that Sinclair was not feathering his own nest." I nodded.

Next to be called to give evidence was a surgeon, Andrew Campbell. Doctor Campbell confirmed that he had visited the dying James Robinson. When Robinson's mother-in-law, who was tending him, left the two men alone together, the doctor asked his patient – "by way of preparing him for the inevitable", as Campbell put it – whether he had written a will. "He said that he had not, because he disliked attorneys," there were a few chuckles as the doctor said this, "and he asked me to help him. In my bag I had a piece of paper with an unwanted letter on one side only, and on the other side I wrote as Mr Robinson spoke. When he had finished I read it back to him; he said it was as he wished, and I held it for him to sign. I promised him that I would take it to an attorney and get a proper will drawn from it."

The young man at the lawyers' table – James Garnham, according to Wilson's notes – nodded. "And did your patient, sir, seem to you to be of sound mind and well able to express his wishes?"

The doctor nodded. "His illness was physical – not of the mind. And his pain was not so far advanced as to make him delirious."

"And what happened then, doctor?" asked Garnham.

The doctor cleared his throat. "I meant to call on an attorney the next day, but I was much engaged with other patients, and I did not consider Mr Robinson to be in any imminent danger." He clasped his hands nervously. "It was three days later when I called again on him, and found him to be much worse. His mind had quite gone with fever and pain, sir."

"Indeed. And what did you do about his will?"

"I decided that it would be useless to apply to anyone to make a will, with the testator," he looked questioningly at the lawyer, who nodded, "with the testator no longer able to comprehend it."

"And so the paper you wrote and had signed by Mr Robinson on your earlier visit to him is, in effect, his will," said Garnham. He picked up a piece of paper from the table and handed it to the clerk, who walked to the dock and passed it to the doctor. "Is this that paper?"

Campbell looked at it. "It is, yes."

"And can you see any alteration to it? Since you wrote it and Mr Robinson signed it? Look carefully, if you please."

The doctor did as he was asked and looked again at the paper, turning it to the light and peering closely at it. "No," he said eventually. "This is as it was when I handed it to Mrs Allen – Mr Robinson's mother-in-law. When I called at the house after Mr Robinson's death, I gave it to her, with my sincerest apologies for not having taken it to an attorney in time."

The doctor was released from the dock, and an usher called for the crowd to make room as he escorted a lady to the dock. She was not elderly – about sixty would be my estimate, although I am always careful when guessing a lady's age (or at least when owning to my guess). As she mounted the few stairs and took hold of the rail I could see her hands trembling, but she held her black-bonneted head high and answered the lawyer in clear tones. This was Eliza Allen, mother-in-law to the late Mr Robinson.

"It is hard for a mother to outlive her daughter," she said. "I miss her every day, but it was some consolation that she had married a good man – a fine man – and after her passing he took care of me as well as any son." She blinked rapidly. "And when James – my son-in-law – sickened, I was glad to care for him in my turn."

"Did you know, madam," asked the lawyer, "of Mr Robinson's intention to make out his will in your favour?"

Mrs Allen shook her head. "We never spoke of it, no."

"You knew that Mr Robinson had a brother?"

"I did, yes – a younger brother. And a wickeder, less grateful man never walked this earth. The contrast between the two brothers could not have been greater. James tried to help him, years ago, but he drank, sir, and he gambled, and plenty more besides."

"A rogue, then, madam," said the lawyer, "and moreover a rogue who would simply have squandered any money he might have been left. A fact which his elder brother knew only too well." He looked up at Mrs Allen, who nodded in agreement. He paused – a lawyerly trick I recognised. He waited until the court was almost silent. "And can you tell us, Mrs Allen, the name of this ungrateful and spendthrift younger brother?"

"I can, sir: William Robinson."

Garnham turned to the bench. "As you will see from your papers, my lord, it is William Robinson who brings before you the allegation that the will has been forged by the prisoner." He turned again to look at Mrs Allen. "William Robinson has alleged that the will has been forged by Thomas Sinclair, the man who stands there accused. Do you know Mr Sinclair, madam?"

Mrs Allen nodded. "I do, sir, yes. He has been my neighbour for two years, and we are to be married next month."

There was a moment of silence and then a hubbub of whispering as people digested this revelation.

"Ah," I said. Wilson looked at me and I explained. "It seems that the ne'er-do-well brother wanted to inherit, and when he didn't, he reasoned that people might believe that Mr Sinclair would forge the will in favour of his intended wife. And so he seeks to have the will disregarded, which would leave him, as next of kin, the only beneficiary."

"But what he overlooked," added Wilson, "was that Mr Sinclair's reputation is far better than his own, which will certainly influence the jury."

Just then the man to my left moved further along the bench to allow another to sit down between us: it was Wontner.

"Am I in time for the verdict?" he asked. I nodded. "And has the case been helpful to your deliberations on the nature of forgery?"

"Indeed," I said. "The will was not done before a lawyer but may well still be recognised. And in deciding that, the reputations of those involved contribute much to our belief in an object's genuineness or otherwise."

And as if to prove me right, after deliberating for only a matter of minutes, the foreman of the jury stood to announce that he and his fellows had found Thomas Sinclair not guilty. The old man and Mrs Allen smiled at each other across the courtroom, and I silently wished them much happiness together.

CHAPTER THIRTEEN

The Congress of Vienna

MONDAY 29TH JANUARY 1827 – AFTERNOON

L eaving Wontner speaking to a colleague who had waylaid him, Wilson and I pushed our way out of the courtroom, apologising as we went, and were just drawing a much-needed breath of air out in the street when we heard a halloo behind us. We turned, and there was James Harmer. I had first met him three or four years earlier and since then had grown to admire him enormously. With his zeal for reform in the criminal courts he was undoubtedly a thorn in the side of his fellow lawyers, but his willingness to think deeply about such matters and his unwillingness to accept that because something was so it should remain so had both impressed me.

"Constable Plank," he said warmly, shaking my hand, "and another fine constable," as he shook Wilson's.

"William Wilson, sir," said that fine constable.

"Are you on your way in or out?" asked the lawyer, pointing to the doorway of the Old Bailey.

"Out," I said. "We have just been listening to the trial of a man charged with forging a will."

"Splendid – I am on my way back too, and we shall keep company." And, as was his wont, Harmer simply stepped into the street and held up his hand to halt the coach heading our way. He tipped his hat at the jarvey and led us across as a mother duck would her ducklings. "Forgery, you say. You had an interest?"

"Not an arresting interest, no, but still a professional one. Wilson and I are concerned with the nature of forgery, but in the world of paintings."

"Paintings?" repeated the lawyer as he strode along Skinner Street. For a heavy-set man, he walked with great speed, his breath clouding in the air as he marched on. "What sort of paintings?"

"Miniatures," replied Wilson. "French miniatures."

"French ones, eh?" A church clock struck and Harmer pulled his watch out of his pocket. "My next appointment is not for an hour, and my stomach calls for attention. Would you gentlemen care to join me?" He put his watch back and without waiting for an answer bustled away up

Snow Hill towards the Saracen's Head. Wilson and I followed him.

Once we were all settled within reach of the fire's warmth, a tankard in front of each of us and demands made for a chop apiece, Harmer leaned back in his chair. "French miniatures, you say." I nodded. "Something of a slippery subject these days, French art."

"Because of the wars?" I asked.

"Indeed – and their aftermath." The lawyer took a long draught of his ale. "You remember the Congress of Vienna?" I nodded. He looked at Wilson. "But you are too young, of course; you were barely breeched in 1815. Castlereagh – our foreign secretary at the time – and after him Wellington sat down with the European ambassadors to thrash out what to do next. Most of it concerned portioning out territory so that we would all balance off and remain at peace. We held on to various colonies in Africa and Asia but handed over Java to the Dutch and Martinique to the French. French interests at the negotiating table were represented by a fellow called Talleyrand."

"A crafty fellow," I said. "Lame in the leg, but more than made up for it in the brain." I tapped the side of my head.

Just then the chops arrived and silence descended as we addressed ourselves to them. When we had all finished, and even Wilson could not find a morsel of meat or a spot of gravy left on his plate, the history lesson continued.

"Most of the agreement," said Harmer, pausing to worry at a back tooth with his tongue, "concerned territory, as I said, but there were also long discussions about the restitution of cultural objects." Wilson looked puzzled. "Handing back artworks plundered during the wars," clarified Harmer. "The French were reluctant – after all, the Louvre in Paris had been built expressly to house the proceeds of French looting – but they had to give way. And," he leaned forward in his chair and smiled, "our Prince Regent saw an opportunity."

"The King?" asked Wilson.

"Now, yes – but the old king was still alive in 1815, of course," replied Harmer. "Prinny has always had an eye for luxury, and he thought that some of those lovely things that the French would have to give up would look very well here in London."

I shook my head; I could remember the debate about it at the time, with outraged stories in the newspapers leading to heated arguments in the taverns.

"But surely these things should go back to wherever they were taken from," said Wilson.

"Quite right too," said the lawyer approvingly. "But Prinny told Liverpool, who was prime minister even back then, that he wanted some statues and pictures, and Liverpool passed on this request to Castlereagh. And Castlereagh, fine fellow, pointed out that if we were to take any objects from the Louvre, Britain would be no better than France: we would be taking war plunder. So publicly we could not negotiate to buy anything from the French, and much of it was then returned. Publicly, I say." He tapped the side of his nose.

"But privately?" asked Wilson, leaning forward as he was swept up in the tale.

"Ah well, privately." Harmer shook his head. "Let us say simply that many of our great families have spent the past decade buying as much art as their agents can carry. And the French, with their state coffers almost bare after Napoleon's excesses, are happy to sell. And not just war plunder either, which is why I mention all of this." Harmer drained his tankard and looked disappointedly into it. "You talk of French miniatures, and you spent the morning at a trial for forgery, so I assume that you are concerned about irregularities in the trade in French art." I nodded. "During the wars, it was not only foreign collections that were looted; soldiers, as you can imagine, will take whatever they can from wherever they can. And many noble French families were encouraged to contribute to the war effort – willingly or otherwise. In addition, others are now selling off their treasures to make up for losses suffered. In short, there is plenty of French art on the market, but with so much of it acquired under, shall we say, mysterious circumstances, it can be all but impossible to prove its origin."

"So it may be stolen?" asked Wilson. Harmer nodded. "Or forged?"

The lawyer pulled out his watch again and turned it to the light. "Or forged," he agreed. "And now, gentlemen, I must take my leave. As always, a pleasure to see you." He put some coins on the table and waved away my hand as I tried to contribute. "I am well breeched today, thanks to a client who has most unexpectedly paid his bill – let us all enjoy his generosity."

We all stood and Harmer hurried from the tavern. Wilson and I left at a more leisurely pace, and as we walked along Holborn I pondered. The lawyer had mentioned agents scooping up pieces of art for English clients, and Miss Conant's art tutor Bonneville had made just such an offer to me.

"Wilson," I said, turning to my companion. "How do you fancy playing the part of a rum cull?"

Wilson raised an eyebrow.

CHAPTER FOURTEEN

Lord Nameless goes calling

FRIDAY 9TH FEBRUARY 1827

Nearly a fortnight later, after Miss Conant had delivered a carefully-worded note to Bonneville and he had replied in equally circumspect terms, Wilson and I made our way to the art tutor's "petit studio", as he called it, in Bateman's Buildings – a narrow, dark alleyway running between Soho Square and Queen Street.

"Strange place for an artist," remarked Wilson. "I thought they needed light for their work." He ran a finger around the inside of his high collar. "The sooner I can get out of these ridiculous duds and back into my uniform, the happier I shall be," he muttered.

Wilson's substantial build was a long way from the dandy's spare silhouette, and he found the tight coat and trousers and the starched collar very constricting, even in the very largest sizes that Mr Hunter had been able to find in his storeroom. But perhaps that worked to our advantage: a young man just come into a fortune and in search of some dubious articles for a private collection light well appear uneasy, and with his fidgeting and his grimacing, Wilson gave an excellent impression of unease.

"Don't lurk in the doorway like a constable," I reminded him, "and remember that you have money and so can be careless of people. And nice things – you like nice things." He nodded.

We were about to knock on the dark green door, as instructed in Bonneville's note, but before we could a grimy little maid, no more than twelve, opened it and a man came out. I stepped aside to allow him past but he did not meet my eye or even acknowledge me and simply hurried off down the alley, hunched into his coat. The maid beckoned us in and led us up three flights of stairs to the attic. She pushed open the door and stood aside. "Two gen'lemen," she said and then disappeared back downstairs.

Bonneville was standing at an easel, lit from behind by a good-sized window. He laid down the brush he was holding and wiped his hands on a cloth hanging from the easel, taking care to drape it over his work before leaving it.

"My friend from the gallery," he said, coming towards us, "and a friend of his."

I shook his hand. "John Snaith, sir," I said, and then turned to indicate Wilson. "This is… as you say, a friend of mine. It is perhaps best for all concerned if we keep his name out of this for now."

Wilson stepped forward and looked down at the Frenchman with supreme disinterest. "Nameless – let us say George Nameless, shall we?" I blinked; I had never heard Wilson speak in such refined tones, but he obviously had an excellent ear for mimicry.

"Mr Nameless it is," replied Bonneville.

"Lord Nameless, actually," said Wilson. "Since dear papa…" he drew a handkerchief, with some difficulty, from the pocket of his tight waistcoat and dabbed at his eye.

I spoke quickly before Wilson's acting talents were exhausted. "I have known Lord… Nameless for many years, having had the honour of representing his late father," here Wilson nodded sorrowfully and dabbed again, "in some matters of business. When I spoke to his Lordship of our meeting at the gallery, and mentioned that you might be able to acquire certain items, he asked me to effect an introduction."

Wilson interrupted me. "I wanted to ensure that my particular requirements are clearly understood," he said, looking around the studio. "Papa's art collection – my art collection now – is somewhat dull. Valuable, of course, but one can tire quickly of hills and horses. My own tastes are rather more – Continental." He smiled roguishly. "Do we understand each other, sir?"

I imagined rather than saw Bonneville rubbing his hands, but the anticipation of riches was clear in his voice. "We do, sir, most assuredly." The Frenchman then made a dumb play of regret, shrugging his shoulders and turning down the corners of his mouth. "But, hélas! Such tastes are difficult to satisfy. These pieces are not, as you say, hills and horses, and there are certain obstacles to creating them. You need artists with a specific talent, and ladies willing to be immortalised. The risk involved for all concerned demands a certain... price premium." He paused and looked shrewdly at his target.

Wilson, or rather Lord Nameless, fell willingly into his trap. "Do what you must, sir, for I will have my paintings. Send word to Snaith and he will take care of things." He sighed deeply as though bored, and wandered over to gaze out of the window.

I took out my notebook, taking care that the Frenchman should not see anything written in it.

"I assume that there will be expenses to be paid up front, to secure the particular expertise you mention," I said, pencil poised. "The name of your banker, sir?" Bonneville hesitated. "If we hurry," I continued, "we can arrange a payment this very afternoon."

His avarice made the decision for him. "Renard," he said. "Craven Street."

Sam Plank's schooldays

THURSDAY 15TH FEBRUARY 1827 – MORNING

The next Thursday I was sitting in the back room at Great Marlborough Street, waiting for any warrants that might be issued. Wilson was already out on one; since the beginning of the year, I had allowed him to see to the less contentious warrants on his own, and this morning's involved a rogue who knew the system well and was unlikely to cause trouble. Physical trouble, of course, Wilson could handle well, but if someone was argumentative or cunning or otherwise slippery, a more experienced constable might be needed.

As I smoothed out the previous evening's newspaper on the table, Thomas Neale the office-keeper put his head round the door.

"Someone to see you, Sam." He glanced back over his shoulder. "In private. Delicate matter. Says he knows you and wants to speak only to you. Seems respectable enough – smart dress."

I folded the newspaper and stood. "Bring him in here, Tom."

The office-keeper disappeared, and a few moments later there was a knock at the door and in came a man of about my own age, dressed, as Tom had said, smartly, in a dark coat with gleaming buttons. He took off his hat and held out his hand.

"Sam Plank," he said. "I would have known you any-where." He smiled at me. "Imagine me without these," he pointed to his side whiskers, "and with holes in the knees of my trousers."

"Ben Sharpe," I said, shaking his hand now with a deal more welcome and conviction. "Heavens above – it must be thirty years." I indicated a chair and my visitor sat.

"A little more, even," he said. "My knuckles still smart sometimes, when I remember old Batey's ruler, but with-out that start in life, I daresay we'd both be hauling sacks on the river – or dead by now, like my father."

"And mine," I added. "Mr Bateman – I haven't thought of him for years. I wonder what became of him." I shook my head. "Probably went to his grave quizzing the diggers on how they had calculated the size of the hole for his coffin."

"So here you are, a constable," said Sharpe, indicating our surroundings. "And making a success of it, from what I hear."

"Hear?" I repeated. "From whom?"

"We both of us work for justice, Sam, you and I. All the multiplication tables that old Batey drilled into us have come in handy for me: I work at Custom House. Specifically, I am one of the comptrollers of accounts in the Warehousing Department, with particular responsibility for London Docks." He touched his hand to his heart and bowed his head in jesting respect.

"You have risen high, to be overseeing so much trade," I said. "Do I take it, then, that you are come to see me on a matter of business?"

My visitor shifted in his seat and leaned forward. "Have you heard of the vaults beneath London Docks?" I nodded. "We use them to store wine and spirits – brandy and the like," he continued. "They are kept very secure, with guards and gatekeepers on duty day and night."

"And there has been a theft?" I asked. "But surely the river police…"

Sharpe held up a hand to stop me. "It is not a theft – something rather more delicate than that, and for this

reason I need a fresh eye on the matter. A fresh and experienced eye. I do not want stories and speculation to
circulate, and you know how river folk like to gossip."
Brought up like me in the dank and dripping alleyways of
Wapping, Ben Sharpe would remember how news –
good or evil – would leap from window to window, from
tavern to tavern, often beating its very subject to his des-
tination. "The gatekeeper who was on duty last night
came to see me first thing this morning; one of his watchmen had found something. Something out of the ordi-
nary. A trusted man is now standing guard. Will you
come, Sam? I have a coach waiting outside."

Our coach rattled down Regent Street, around the Quadrant and on into Pall Mall. We barely slowed at Charing
Cross and continued at a dizzying pace along the Strand,
through Fleet Street and then plunged southwards again
at Bridge Street. Just short of Chatham Place and Black-
friars Bridge we turned left; ahead of us was the magnificent bulk of Custom House. The coach slowed as we
approached, but my companion knocked on the ceiling
and called out to the driver to continue. Past the looming
shadow of the Tower we hurried, and into the road sep-
arating the Royal Mint on the left from the docks on the
right.

"They make it," said Sharpe, pointing to the mint, "and they spend it." Here he pointed to the docks, smiling grimly.

Now we were forced to move at a more careful pace, as carts and barrows and wagons swarmed around us. The noise was terrific, with wheels squealing, men shouting, horses neighing, boxes crashing and warning bells ringing. We inched our way along Pennington Street, the forbidding brick wall of the docks rearing up alongside us, and finally the coach drew to a halt outside a large – and firmly closed – wooden gate.

"Come," said my companion, and we descended from the coach. I felt relieved to be on solid ground once more, after our breakneck journey. At the gate Sharpe knocked and called, and with a great creaking it was hauled open a mere sliver. A small man with a curious face peered out at us, and when he caught sight of my companion he quickly let us in, leaning against the gate to close it securely once again and shooting home an enormous bolt.

"Come," said Sharpe again, and I followed him across the narrow courtyard and into the warehouse. Two storeys high and made of expanses of brickwork broken with stone plinths and patterns suggestive of the sea, it stretched almost as far as I could see. Inside, we went through another carefully-guarded door and finally found ourselves in a vast storeroom, piled with boxes, crates, bundles and sacks.

"A bonded warehouse," explained Sharpe as we walked quickly along a central aisle. "Goods are retained here until the duty owed is paid." We reached another guarded door; once through there we descended a staircase and went through yet another guarded door. "And down here," said Sharpe, standing back to let me take a look, "are the vaults."

The smell almost made my eyes water – a mixture of fumes from the wine and rum, and the fungous stench of dry rot. The floor was sticky, as if newly tarred.

"Sugar," said Sharpe, "seeping from the barrels."

My eyes gradually adjusted to the gloom, and then a most astonishing sight greeted me. Stretching off into the distance were dozens – perhaps even hundreds – of curved brick vaults, stepping away from me like leaping waves. Lamps hung from some of the arches, throwing deep shadows around the place, and piled up in quantities too numerous to count were casks, pipes, barrels, hogsheads and butts.

"Brandy, sherry, port, wine and rum," said Sharpe. "Coming from all corners of the world and heading to all corners of the world, and every drop of it passing through London and paying us for the privilege. In these vaults we keep it at a stable temperature, and secure. You noticed the locked and guarded doors."

I nodded. "We have passed through four to reach this point."

"And this is what makes no sense," said Sharpe as he turned off the main aisle and into a more secluded part of the vault. "Look."

We stopped and there, hanging from a bracket at the top point of an arch, twisting slowly and casting alternate long and short shadows across the face of the man guarding it, was a body.

"One of the watchmen found him this morning, just like this," said Sharpe sadly. "There was no rush to cut him down – he was long dead. He is one of ours, Plank – one of our men." He turned to the guard. "The letter, please." The man handed Sharpe a folded piece of paper and then stepped back into the shadows. "We found this in his coat pocket," said Sharpe, passing the paper to me, and I walked to the nearest lamp to read it.

"To my fellow officers," it said. "Please forgive me. I owe too much – my debt is too great. I can endure no longer. Robert King."

I looked across at Sharpe. "It is his hand?" I asked. He nodded. "So self-murder," I said.

"So it would seem, but..."

I walked over to my old friend. "But it does not fit with the man?"

Sharpe shook his head. "King liked to gamble, as do many, but for entertainment only. He was clever with numbers – you have to be, to work here. He was one of our best officers. And a man who knows his mathematics and can work out the odds would not allow his debt to become unendurable."

"Did Mr King work down here in the vaults?" I asked, stepping closer to the body. King was in his early thirties, I guessed, and in good physical condition – death aside, of course.

"No – upstairs."

"But he would have had free access to the vaults?"

"Certainly: as a customs officer, he could go anywhere in the docks."

"And apart from customs officers, who else can come down here?" I asked.

"Merchants like to use the premises to show off their stock and to entice new customers," said Sharpe. "They can apply for tasting permits to hand out to guests, who can then come down here to sample the wines and liquors. Very popular those permits are, as you can imagine."

"We shall need a list of any such permits that were presented yesterday evening," I said. Sharpe nodded at the man in the shadows, and he walked off.

"You think that someone else was involved, then?" he asked me. "You also doubt self-murder?"

"I do," I said, "but not for the same reason. How high do you think that noose is from the ground? Seven feet? Eight?"

"About that, yes."

"And this is how he was found – nothing has been moved?"

"Just as you see it," said Sharpe.

"So how did Mr King get up there without a stool?"

CHAPTER SIXTEEN

The widower's room

THURSDAY 15TH FEBRUARY 1827 –
AFTERNOON

A s I looked around Robert King's lodgings, I thought – and not for the first time – that we men make a poor show of housekeeping. As he had handed me the scrap of paper with King's address on it, Sharpe had warned me not to expect much.

"He was a widower," he had said, jerking his head towards the body that was just then being lowered to the ground by three men. "His wife died in childbirth, oh, ten years ago now, and he never remarried. Women, yes, apparently, but not to live in."

The landlady was an incurious creature who simply directed me to King's room on the first floor of the building in Chapman Street, a ten-minute walk from the docks, and left me to look around. It was tidy enough; as befitted a man who made his living from checking and recording, King obviously disliked clutter and mess. In the cupboard were two shirts and his underclothes, while the bedding had been pulled up and straightened on the sagging bedstead near the window and the pot beneath it was empty. The hearth had been cleared. There was a small table and chair in the corner, and on the table was a clean plate and tumbler, a pile of papers and a book. I picked it up: Defoe's "Colonel Jack". A ribbon marked King's place, about a third of the way through. The topmost paper on the pile beneath the book caught my eye; it was a Custom House receipt. I picked it up and went over to the window to read it.

I had seen a few such receipts before; they are printed by Custom House, with spaces for details of the ship and its cargo to be filled in and for the captain to obtain the required signatures once duty had been paid. What was strange about this one was that none of the spaces had been filled in, except for the signature of the officer who had apparently put the record into the register at Custom House – a J Morgan. I returned to the pile of papers: there were five more identical documents, each incomplete apart from the signature of Mr Morgan.

I went downstairs and walked into the dingy yard at the back of the building where the landlady was thumping a sodden cloth against a washboard. She stood upright when she saw me, holding her red hands to the small of her back and stretching.

I indicated the papers in my hand. "Mr King died this morning, at work. I am taking these papers to assist with our enquiries."

If I expected any show of distress or sympathy, I was to be disappointed.

"Take what you like," she said, shrugging. "He was three weeks behind on the rent, so whatever's left in there I'll take in payment. Papers are no use to me." She bent once more to her work and I left her to it. I was glad that I had slipped the Defoe into my pocket; it was one that Martha and I had yet to read.

It was a long walk home but I was thankful, as I always am after attending a corpse, to be walking upright and not lying on my back in a cold room, waiting for burial. By coincidence, Martha was also doing the washing in the yard, her arms red from the water, the clean linen pegged up behind her on the line that she looped from nail to nail like a cat's cradle on washdays. She too stood and stretched, her hands at her back, but her face was far from indifferent when she saw me.

"Sam," she said with a warm smile, "you're home early. And just in time: you can empty the tub for me."

After I had tipped out the water into the gutter and left the tub propped up against the wall to drain, I went back into the kitchen. Martha was sitting at the table, gulping down a tumbler of barley water and looking at the papers I had brought in. I poured myself a drink from the jug and sat beside her. Her skin was glistening from the effort and the steam, and one of her curls was stuck in a perfect spiral to the side of her neck. I leaned across and kissed it and she tutted, but I could tell that she was pleased.

"What are these?" she asked. "Are you running errands for the customs men now?"

I explained how I had spent the morning. As I described the body hanging in the vault, my soft-hearted wife shook her head.

"Poor man," she said. "Does he leave a family?"

I told her about the widower's sad little lodging in Chapman Street. She picked up the book that King had been reading and looked at me.

"An adventure story," I said. "About a young pickpocket who goes to the colonies and becomes a reformed character." I reached over and put my hand on hers. "We shall read it together, in memory of Mr King."

Martha nodded and gave me a small smile. "And his papers?"

"Well, these are receipts from Custom House," I said, pulling one of the papers towards me. "When a ship arrives in London, it moors outside Custom House – you know that grand building – and the captain goes inside to declare his cargo and have it assessed for excise duties. He then sails into the secure dock and arranges to have the cargo unloaded and checked – weighed and gauged and the like. The vault I was in this morning is where brandy, rum and other spirits are stored until the duty is paid and they are cleared for sale. Once the captain has paid the duty to the collector and it has been checked and approved by the comptroller, he goes back to Custom House with their cocket – their receipt – as proof of payment, and it is all entered in the register. This," I tapped the paper with my finger, "is the final receipt the captain receives, a record of that entry in the register."

Martha frowned slightly. "And Mr King – he was responsible for putting those entries in the register?"

"No," I said, "and that is what's puzzling me. King was a comptroller in the vaults – he checked the duties collected by the collectors against the volumes recorded by the gaugers."

"So why did he have these papers?" asked Martha. "What use would they be to him?"

"None at all to him, but perhaps to someone else..." I said. "Let's look again: what does the receipt actually record?"

Martha looked carefully at the paper in front of her. "There are spaces to write the date on which the entry was made in the register, the name of the ship, its home port, the name of the captain, where it had sailed from and the date on which it arrived in London. Then there is an undertaking that all duties have been paid, and space against that for the signatures of two officers – perhaps the collector and the comptroller – and then that of the captain. Finally there is a space for the signature of the Custom House officer who makes the entry in the register. And that is the only signature already completed." She looked up at me.

Something occurred to me. "But no detail about the actual cargo?"

Martha checked again, running her finger down the paper. She shook her head. "No: it simply confirms that the ship was 'cleared of her cargo and rummaged by the tide surveyors'. Rummaged?"

"To check for anything hidden in secret compartments and smuggled in without paying duty," I explained. "So all that this receipt can provide by way of information is the name, home port and captain of the ship – all of which can be found out elsewhere – and where its cargo was loaded."

"And that duty was paid, and everything has been checked to the satisfaction of Custom House," added Martha.

I nodded slowly. "That everything is as it should be." It was certainly puzzling.

CHAPTER SEVENTEEN

Fourteen frames

TUESDAY 20TH FEBRUARY 1827

"Look, here," said Wilson, jabbing a finger at the newspaper on the table. I glanced at it as I shrugged out of my coat – *The Times.* "Thank heavens I spotted it – the paper is several days old. Look."

"A moment, if you please," I said, turning to hang up my hat. Instances like this reminded me that Wilson, for all his height and broad shoulders, was still a young man, and he hopped from foot to foot with impatience. With exaggerated care I sat at the table and pulled the paper towards me.

"An auction of the stock of a jewellery and gold business…" I leaned closer to read the small print, "on the Strand. This morning." I looked up at Wilson. "Are you hoping to buy a trinket for a sweetheart?"

Wilson almost rolled his eyes but caught himself in time. "Read on, sir," he said. "Look at the stock they list."

I read aloud. "The entire and valuable stock consists of a complete and judicious assortment of the best manufactured jewellery, in brilliants, emerald, ruby, opal, and other necklaces, lockets, crosses, brooches, rings, earrings, armlets, bracelets, gold chased miniature frames, eye-glasses..." I stopped and looked again. "Miniature frames."

The notice in the paper had said that the auction would be starting at eleven, and the little shop on the corner of Adam Street on the south side of the Strand was already crowded when we arrived at a quarter to the hour. People seem to enjoy picking over the remnants of a business or indeed a life; there had been much excitement, I recalled, when it was announced that the personal and household effects of the late Duke of York would be auctioned at Mr Christie's Room in King Street at the end of the month, with even Martha spending a happy evening speculating about what might be on display.

Seeing the throng at the shop, I had no wish to be trapped or observed inside the premises, so Wilson stood across the road to see who came and went while I feigned an interest in the wine merchant next door. We had both worn plain coats, for which I was extremely grateful when Wilson whistled to catch my attention and jerked his head to indicate the man walking briskly from the direction of Somerset House. In his flowing gown and with that shock of grey hair, it was unmistakably Bonneville. I quickly raised the newspaper to hide my face from him as he passed. As a nearby church tolled the hour, I lowered the paper just in time to see the art tutor welcomed by the auctioneers with a loud hulloo; he was obviously well-known to them.

With Bonneville at the auction I certainly could not risk being recognised, and so I beckoned to Wilson to join me and we walked a little way up the Strand. From a few doors along we watched yet more people arrive for the auction, and we could hear the occasional call or bark of laughter as the lots were announced, displayed and sold. After little more than half an hour – for which I was grateful, as the skies had darkened threateningly – Bonneville swept out of the jeweller's shop and strode off back towards Somerset House. As we had agreed, Wilson went into the auction while I followed Bonneville at a safe distance.

I almost lost him, as while I stayed on the south side of the Strand he quickly crossed to the north and then immediately turned into Southampton Street, heading for Covent Garden. The market had all but finished for the day, and the streets were crowded with carts and wagons being loaded with empty baskets by weary traders. Peering around the corner I saw Bonneville making for the colonnaded porch of the market building; once safely under cover, sheltering from the rain that was now falling steadily, he looked up at the blue clock on St Paul's, turned up his collar against the chill wind, and waited.

Taking care to conceal myself as I did so, I walked carefully around the edge of the square, crossed the cobbled yard, and ducked under the porch of the market building on the opposite side to where Bonneville was standing. I walked swiftly along two sides of the building until I was just around the corner from him; anyone watching would have been amused to see me peep around at him and then rear back when I saw that I was only a matter of two yards from him. Thankfully he had his back to me, and moreover was preoccupied with watching a shapely farmer's wife bending over to sort through her bushels of apples.

The church bell started to sound noon, and Bonneville pulled his watch out of one of his deep cloak pockets to check it, glancing up in the direction of Henrietta Street. He spotted someone and raised his hand in greeting, dropping his watch back into his pocket. Walking towards him was the oldest bank clerk I had ever seen in my life – Renard's man.

The two shook hands, and the clerk came under the shelter of the porch, brushing the rain from the shoulders of his black coat. I thanked the heavens for the inclement weather, as otherwise they might have conducted their business while strolling about.

"Monsieur Bonneville," said the clerk.

"Mr Greenwood," replied the Frenchman. "You are well, I trust."

The clerk shrugged. "I am nearly eighty years of age, monsieur – but I have my legs and my wits." He looked up at the art tutor. "Was this morning's excursion successful?"

"It was," said Bonneville. "I have secured what is needed for the next consignment. Fourteen frames, all gold."

"Fourteen?" The clerk sounded pleased. "More than enough. Where are they now?"

"They will be delivered to me tomorrow, and I will send them on to you at the bank."

Greenwood the clerk shook his head. "Not this time, no. Renard says that this time they are to go direct to Lagrange. With those constables sniffing about, we want nothing more on the premises."

"A wise precaution," said Bonneville. "And where is Lagrange?"

"We will send word to him this afternoon, and he will let you know where to send the frames." Greenwood peered up at the sky and held out a hand from under the porch. "It seems to have lessened. I will take advantage and my leave." And he set off back down towards the

Strand, at a pace I hope I can match at his age. I waited a moment to allow Bonneville to leave; I did not want to risk walking past him and preferred to keep him ahead of me. He pulled out his watch again, and a slip of paper fell from his pocket. He glanced down at it and then walked off. I was about to dart forward and retrieve it up when a man in a dark coat, collar turned up against the rain, walked past me, bent to pick up the note almost without breaking stride, put it into his pocket and disappeared into Tavistock Court.

Wilson was waiting for me at Great Marlborough Street, his notebook open on the table in the back office. He gnawed impatiently at a fingernail while I took off my coat. I nodded and he began.

"I went into the shop and spoke to one of the porters – they are responsible for showing the items as they are auctioned, and then for packing and delivering them afterwards." He looked up at me and I nodded again. "After I had made a small contribution to his funds, he said that he knew Bonneville – had seen him at other auctions – and that whenever they had miniature frames for sale, they knew that he would turn up."

"Did he ever buy anything else?"

"Once or twice, the fellow said, but not often. And always French paintings if he did buy anything. But miniature frames – he would buy as many of those as they had for sale."

"And are the frames empty?" I asked.

"At this auction, yes. The porter showed them to me: all just frames."

"And Bonneville bought fourteen of them?"

Wilson's head snapped back in surprise. "How did you know that?"

I touched the side of my nose, but then took pity on him and explained what I had overheard in Covent Garden.

"The old clerk from Renard's bank? Greenway, was it? I think Sylvie – Miss Renard – has mentioned him." Wilson flushed slightly at the mention of the young woman.

"Greenwood," I replied. I leaned forward. "So why, do we think, is Bonneville buying up all the miniature frames he can find, and passing them on to Lagrange? And who was the man who picked up the paper that Bonneville dropped?"

Wilson frowned. "Perhaps the miniatures that Lagrange finds in France sometimes have damaged frames? Or ugly frames? And he replaces them before selling the paintings. And the man is most likely another agent acting for a customer, taking careful precautions that no-one knows of his business with Bonneville."

"Perhaps," I said. "We need to know more about these miniatures and how they are acquired. I think maybe Lord Nameless needs to grow a little impatient, and start demanding that addition to his collection."

CHAPTER EIGHTEEN

A proud Englishman

FRIDAY 23RD FEBRUARY 1827

The next morning no sooner had I stepped into the front office at Great Marlborough Street, stamping the snow from my boots, than Thomas Neale beckoned me over. It was early – only just gone eight – so it could not be a warrant, and indeed the amused look on Tom's face suggested that, rather than duty, he had instead the latest *on dit* to share.

He leaned confidentially over the counter, looked quickly down the corridor to check that no-one was there, and said quietly, "Young Wilson. Have you noticed anything," here the office keeper waved a hand in front of his own face, "different about him recently?"

"Different?" I repeated. "Different in what way?"

"More careful," said Tom. He paused. "More barbered. Like a man who is courting."

"Courting!" I almost barked the word. "But he's only..." I stopped as my thoughts caught up with my words. "He's nearly twenty-two."

Tom nodded slowly. "And when you married the inestimable Mrs Plank, you were..."

"Twenty-two." I stood upright. "But I was an independent man, with no responsibilities – I could take a wife when I wanted. Wilson has a widowed mother and several siblings to care for."

"And so a wife would be of great help," said Tom.

"A wife like Mrs Neale, you mean," I said mischievously.

"It would be astonishing bad luck to find another wife like mine," said Tom, smiling grimly. "One like yours, well, she would be a wife worth pursuing."

I couldn't argue with that. "But why mention this now?" I asked. "Has Wilson said something?"

Tom laughed. "Come, Sam – when you were his age, would you have told old fellows like us that you were courting?" He shook his head. "But one advantage of being our age is that you know the signs." He peered down the corridor again. "He's already in – arrived a half-hour ago. So that's sign one: waking early. Sign two: he's had his whiskers trimmed and I caught a generous whiff of pomade."

Just then the door of the back office opened and Wilson himself came out. He saw me and smiled, walking up the corridor towards us.

"Good morning, sir," he said brightly. "Did you happen to walk through Fitzroy Square this morning and see the snow on the trees? A magical sight."

I glanced at Tom; he raised an eyebrow and then wordlessly mouthed, "Sign three."

Alerted by the message I had sent home, Martha met us at the door, her shawl over her shoulders.

"You go on in, William, and help yourself to a slice of bread – not too much, mind, as dinner is nearly ready, but just enough to keep you going. I want a word with Sam." She pulled the door to behind Wilson, and shepherded me back to the yard gate. "Has he said anything?" she asked urgently, looking over her shoulder.

I tried not to smile. "Not a word, no. But he did comment on the pretty trees again, and he's certainly in a good mood, so I think Tom may be right."

"And?" she asked.

"And what?"

Martha rolled her eyes. "And what do we think about it?"

I shrugged. "Does it matter what we think about it? He is a grown man – he can make his own choice."

My wife put her hands on her hips. "His own choice? Sam, you can be remarkably dense at times. Since when did any man make his own choice of a wife? It is the wife who chooses, not the man, and I want to know who is choosing William. Now hurry up and come in, or he will start to wonder."

I considered pointing out that it was she, not I, who had delayed our entry into the house, but decided against it. She was in determined mood this evening, and getting in her path would be unwise and almost certainly painful.

"So, William," said Martha lightly, her back to us as she tidied up after dinner, "I understand that you have become fond of a young woman."

Wilson's eyes opened wide; he looked at me and I shrugged and shook my head, hoping to convince him that I was as surprised as he at the turn the conversation had taken.

He swallowed hard and then squared his shoulders. "I have, Mrs Plank."

Martha turned and stood leaning against the cupboard and wiping her hands on a cloth. Her casual stance did not fool me for a second, but perhaps Wilson was reassured.

"And she is fond of you?"

Wilson flushed a little and nodded. "I believe so, yes."

Martha continued drying her hands for far longer than was necessary. "But you have been a gentleman towards her?" She looked steadily at Wilson and now her hands were still.

"Yes, Mrs Plank."

"And you hope to make her your wife?"

It was a question I would never have dared ask, but I found myself curious to hear the answer.

Wilson was silent for perhaps a minute before saying, "I think so, one day, yes. But there are... difficulties. She is not entirely free to marry." One of us must have looked shocked, because Wilson half-laughed and continued quickly. "Oh no, she is not married already – but neither is she entirely free."

Martha looked at me and I could see the smile in her eyes. I knew that she had for many months nurtured a hope that Wilson would marry Alice, the young unmarried mother whom we had taken into our home about a year previously, before finding her and her infant daughter a good position at a coaching inn in Holborn. Alice and Wilson were friends, I knew that, but Alice was still so young, not yet sixteen. But motherhood had matured her beyond her years, so perhaps she was ready to be a wife.

"You would not be the first to bring up another man's child as his own," said Martha.

Wilson frowned.

Martha continued. "And this is a special circumstance, surely. Alice cannot be held responsible for..." her voice trailed off as she saw Wilson shaking his head.

"It is not Alice, Mrs Plank. I am fond of her, of course, but not as a wife – more as a sister." I looked at Martha, and admired the effort of will that kept the disappointment from her face. "No, not Alice. But you have met the woman I mean, sir." Wilson looked at me and smiled. "Miss Renard. Sylvie."

"Ah," I said. Martha was looking at me. "The banker's daughter," I explained to her. "The French one."

"La fille française," said Martha.

"But you said that Miss Renard is not entirely free," I reminded Wilson.

"She may not have a husband," he said with a shade of bitterness in his voice, "but she certainly has a father."

"Indeed she does," I said. "I told you of him, Martha – large, bearded, perhaps a little too..." I patted my own stomach. "His banking house is near Charing Cross."

"Craven Street," said Wilson. "I was hoping to call on him soon. But Sylvie – Miss Renard – seems to think it will do no good. I am not what he wants for her." He looked down at his hands.

Martha bristled, her disappointment now replaced by outrage. "Not what he wants for her? A fine, handsome, decent constable, with excellent prospects and a good heart?" Wilson made to protest, but my wife held up her hand and he fell silent. "So just what is it that this banker – this Frenchman – wants for his daughter?"

Wilson looked up at us, misery on his face. "This Frenchman wants another Frenchman. He may live in England, says Sylvie, and he may speak English, but he is a proud Frenchman and he wants his daughter to marry another proud Frenchman. I can change many things for her – I would happily change many things for her – but where I was born," he shook his head, "there is nothing to be done about that."

Martha was still indignant as we readied ourselves for bed.

"A proud Frenchman, indeed," she said, running her hands over her head and pulling out the pins one by one. "Happy enough to live here, and to serve English clients at that bank of his, and to enjoy all that London has to offer now that France is on its knees..." She turned and looked at me as though it was my fault. "Stays, Sam – do I need to ask?" Once I had unlaced her, she yanked her nightdress over her head and gave her pillow a good, hard pummelling before she slid under the covers. "Proud Frenchman!" she said again. "Someone needs to remind him that a proud Englishman is worth every bit as much. More, in fact." She looked at me expectantly.

I shook my head. "Oh no, not me," I said quickly. "I am not going to Renard to plead Wilson's case, and no more would Wilson thank me for doing it. Your father didn't think much of me, if you recall, but what would he have thought – and, more to the point, what would you have thought – if I had compounded the problem by sending someone else to speak on my behalf?"

"Hmmph," said Martha, but I could tell from the softening of her face that my comparison had hit home. I lifted my arm, and my wife moved across and laid her head on my chest. "I am so very fond of William," she said indistinctly, "and I want to see him settled and happy. I had hopes for Alice, but if this Miss Renard is the one he has chosen..." She sighed.

I rolled my eyes but thankfully she could not see me; she seemed to have forgotten her own earlier declaration that it is the woman who does the choosing. "I am going to visit Bonneville – the art tutor – again soon," I said. "He knows Renard. I will see if I can find out anything more that might help Wilson. And in any case, the lad has known Miss Renard barely a month – his ardour may burn itself out as quickly as it has ignited."

Martha reached up and kissed my cheek, and I knew that I had been forgiven for whatever it was that I had done wrong.

CHAPTER NINETEEN

Clerk of the Second Class

MONDAY 26TH FEBRUARY 1827

I am never more proud of being an Englishman – a Londoner – than when I visit one of our magnificent buildings. To be sure, the construction of Custom House did not go entirely smoothly: when the decision was made to replace the outgrown building with a much grander one next door, the old structure promptly caught fire, as if in a sulk. That was in 1814, and a square toes like me can still remember the explosions as the gunpowder and spirits stored underneath it caught light. Paper fell from the sky like leaves in autumn, as far away as Hackney Marshes. The new Custom House was certainly ambitious in scale, with the surveyor's plans calling for a river frontage of nearly four hundred and fifty feet – and fireproof cellars. Unfortunately the builders, with an eye to their profit, put in only half the foundations they had promised, and two years ago the timber pilings gave way under the strain. It made quite a stink, prompting questions in Parliament, and the Chancellor himself called it a scandalous fraud. But London could not be without its Custom House, and so the central section was speedily rebuilt with firmer foundations and a third row of very graceful columns, and it was to this vast and glorious building that I turned my step today.

I explained my business to the man at the door; with his eye trained to tell sailors from captains and collectors from comptrollers, he quickly took in my constable's uniform and questioned me no further. At his direction, I walked across the grand entrance hall and turned into a corridor thronged with people. "Follow the horde," he had said, and so I did. We went past a few large wooden doors, one or two ajar to show bustling offices within, and then up a wide double staircase. From the first floor, tall windows looked out onto the river, and several people stood and gazed at the spectacle. If anyone should ask the source of London's wealth and power, well, here it was, laid out before us. But with business to complete, I watched for only a minute before once more joining the flow of people heading to the Long Room.

The name is well chosen for this enormous space. I am told it is nearly five hundred feet in length and a hundred feet wide, and it is the workplace for seven hundred clerks and officers and a thousand tide-waiters and servants. A gently curved ceiling vaulted overhead, at least four times the height of a man, and light filled the room from more tall windows giving onto the river. I stood for a moment to get my bearings and then crossed the room to one of the high desks set under those great windows. I showed the clerk sitting there my papers, and he pointed down the row of desks to one at the far end. I pushed my way through the crowds – some were there for business, clutching papers like mine, but many more were there to gawp – until I reached the desk he had indicated.

Sitting behind it on a tall stool was an exceedingly thin man. His upper body in its severe black coat was thin, with his shoulders and elbows forming sharp angles, his face behind its spectacles was thin and suggested his age to be about thirty, and his hands, one writing in a ledger and the other marking his place on the paper he was copying, were the thinnest of all, with long bony fingers. I waited for a moment and then started to speak, but the clerk held up a thin hand to silence me.

After about three minutes he laid down his pen and looked up at me. Most unexpectedly, he smiled broadly, softening the harsh planes of his face.

"Please forgive my rudeness," he said. "Transcribing must be done with absolute precision – the Long Room brooks no errors in her ledgers." He tapped on the book before him. "This, sir, is a legal record." He looked me up and down. "Although I see, sir, that you are in need of no lecture on the importance of legal documents. You are yourself a man of justice."

I liked the sound of that: a man of justice. "Constable Samuel Plank, of Great Marlborough Street," I said.

"Owen Avery, Clerk of the Second Class." He reached over the desk and we shook hands; his was every bit as bony as it looked. "And as a constable, you are therefore not here to register the arrival of your ship, or to ask for a receipt for the payment of your duties."

"I am not," I agreed. I placed one of my papers on the desk in front of the clerk. He looked down at it and then up at me. "I found this in the lodging of a colleague of yours." Avery's eyes widened slightly but he said nothing. "Not from here in the Long Room, but a customs officer. He worked in the warehouse in Pennington Street. A comptroller." I pointed at the paper. "Is it usual for comptrollers to keep papers like these in their lodgings?"

"He had more than one?" asked Avery, his eyes darting to the other papers I was holding.

"He had several – identical to that one."

Avery adjusted his spectacles and looked down at the paper. "And you want to know…" He stopped and looked up at me.

"Is it a true document?" I asked. "Is it forged? Should he have had it at all?"

Avery bent closer to the document then reached under his desk and brought out a very small bell, which he rang. A young lad walked swiftly over; Avery whispered in his ear and the lad hared off down the Long Room. A few minutes later another clerk came to our desk, and he and Avery both examined the document. They turned from me and spoke quietly for a moment, and the second clerk peered sharply at me a couple of times before walking away. Avery put his hand on the document on his desk and sighed.

"This," he said portentously, "is a true document. The Long Room issues many such to ship's captains. The Long Room issues them," he repeated. "Not comptrollers in the Pennington Street bonded warehouse. The comptroller gives the captain a cocket showing that all duties have been paid; the captain brings that here; the Long Room records it; and armed with the receipt that she then issues," here he tapped the paper in front of him, "the captain can return and order his cargo to be unloaded."

"But this one is blank," I said.

"It is what we call a pro forma document, yes," said Avery. "The Long Room is, as you can see, a very busy place. To save time, she prepares standard documents – like this one – that can be completed later with specific details."

"And do those standard documents include that signature?" I pointed to the bottom of the paper; next to the printed words 'Register of Ship's Clearance' was the neat signature of J Morgan. "That looks to me like something that should be done at the time, when the document is issued."

Avery leaned forward and lowered his voice. "And you would be right, constable: that signature should be completed only once all the other details have been entered into the ledger. But here we have something of an unusual situation, which is why I called my fellow clerk over – to check my recollection." He cleared his throat. "Mr Morgan was not a well man. To keep up with his duties here in the Long Room, he, well, he sometimes used quiet moments to sign documents in readiness for more busy times." Avery shook his head. "This behaviour is not recommended by the Long Room. Not condoned. Not at all." He took a deep breath. "But we must not speak ill of the dead, for Mr Morgan departed this life some eight months ago, God rest his soul." Avery paused for a moment and closed his eyes. "We thought," he continued, opening them again, "that we had retrieved all of the pro formas with his signature on them and destroyed them, but I always feared that there were some missing.

And it appears that I was right. As you can imagine, a blank document like this that can be completed at will would be worth a deal of money in the wrong hands." He shook his head sadly. "An embarrassment for the Long Room, constable – it will distress her greatly."

"And why, Mr Avery, do you think a comptroller would want to be able to issue such a receipt at will?"

Avery closed his eyes again and swallowed hard. He climbed down off his stool and walked round the desk to stand next to me. He turned to me and whispered into my ear, "Smuggling." He looked at me and smiled sadly. "May the Long Room forgive me for uttering the word."

"Smuggling is a matter for the river police," said Mr Conant as I told him of my day's work.

"Indeed," I agreed, "although I am not looking forward to visiting their office at Wapping New Stairs to share this information with them." Conant looked at me sympathetically; he knew how reluctant I was to visit the part of London where I had grown up. He picked up a decanter and waved it at me but I shook my head; Martha had commented a few nights earlier about the smell of the tavern on my breath, and I knew that the memory of a drunken man in the house unsettled her. We both of us, it seems, prefer to forget our past.

"And yet?" said Conant as he settled into his chair by the fireplace. He looked up at me with amusement. "A magistrate learns to read faces, Sam, and yours tells me that this is not the end of the matter. Come." He indicated the chair opposite him and I sat down.

"The death, sir – of King, the comptroller. Found hanging in the vaults. Apparently self-murder."

Conant sipped his drink. "Guilt?" he suggested. "Fear of being found out? Blackmail payments that he could no longer meet? Despair over a woman?"

"All good explanations for self-murder," I said. "But it troubles me. The lack of a stool. And at King's lodgings – everything was tidied, ready for supper that evening. His place marked in his book. What man, knowing that he is to kill himself that day, bothers to lay the table and mark his place in a book?"

"Murder, then," said Conant.

I nodded. "Murder made to look like self-murder. His killer did not want simply to be rid of King; he wanted all suspicion to fall on King. For the death, for the smuggling and for the forging of the receipts. With a body, the note in the pocket, and evidence of corruption in the form of those signed Custom House documents, the murderer hopes that we will stop looking."

King's death haunted me that evening – a sure sign that I was uneasy about trusting what I had been told. I went to bed but could not settle, turning and sighing until, just after eleven, Martha sat up.

"Samuel," she said, "will you please go downstairs, put on your coat, walk to the corner and whistle for a lad."

"You mean a message lad?" I asked.

"Of course I mean a message lad," she said, pushing against me to heave me towards the edge of the bed. "Send a note to Mr Sharpe, arranging a meeting with him tomorrow morning, to talk about Mr King. And then you can stop thinking about it and we can both have some peace." I got up. Satisfied, my wife gave her pillow a good thump and settled down again, her back to me. "Now, Sam," she said, "before you send me well and truly mad."

CHAPTER TWENTY

A terrible beating

TUESDAY 27TH FEBRUARY 1827

The next morning I was once again outside the massive wooden gate in Pennington Street. This time, when I knocked, I was not admitted immediately. I had to explain my business to the gatekeeper through the narrow opening he allowed, and then wait outside the closed gate while he went off to check my story. A few minutes later he returned and let me in, directing me to the office just inside the warehouse. A clerk – a customs officer, I supposed – was sitting at a tiny desk, ledgers piled up around him on every surface including the floor. He was a young man, his head a mass of angelic yellow curls, his coat dangling off the back of his chair, his shirt sleeves untidily pushed up to the elbow. He seemed not to notice me so I coughed. He held up an ink-stained hand to silence me and continued writing.

When he had finished he looked up at me, noted my uniform (and doubtless my mature years) and scrambled to his feet.

"Forgive me, constable," he said, "but you know how it is with numbers: stop partway and you forget where you were." He smiled so charmingly that I forgave him immediately.

"No matter, Mr...?" I said.

"Smith," he replied.

"Well, Mr Smith, I am here to see Mr Sharpe, on a matter of some urgency. Is he here?"

"In the warehouse, yes, sir, but not here upstairs. Mr Sharpe arrived some time ago, and went down to the vaults." He stopped and frowned. I narrowed my eyes at him and he continued. "It's just that it was an awfully long time ago – nearly an hour now. His inspection rarely takes that long."

"Inspection?" I asked.

"Oh yes, every morning, first thing. Mr Sharpe comes into the office here then goes down to the vaults to speak to the night watchman and to check that all is well. He goes down at eight and is usually back by half past at the latest. But it's ten to the hour, and I haven't seen him return."

I went down into the vaults – a decision for which Martha would scold me mercilessly later – explaining my business at each guarded door and asking whether Sharpe had been seen coming out. Once my eyes had adjusted to the dim light, I started to look for my friend. I walked along the main row of brick archways, their lanterns casting dizzying light patterns on the curved surfaces. I heard a scuffling sound, but the structure of the vault – the low ceilings, the caves created by the arches – made it difficult to determine its source. I walked on, further into the gloom. Suddenly I heard the distinctive sound of a slap, and then the low growling of voices. I halted for a second, and then crept as quietly as I could towards the sound.

Taking cover behind a high pile of barrels, I peeped round into the far corner of the warehouse. Sitting – no, slumped – on the floor, his back against the wall, was Sharpe. His head was nodding forward at a strange angle, and I feared that the dark mark on his cheek was blood. Standing over him, their backs to me, were three men. They whispered to each other, then one of them crouched down and pulled Sharpe's head up by the hair.

"For the last time: we're telling you to leave it alone," he said. "King's death was self-murder – is that clear?"

I held my breath. Sharpe looked up at the man; I could see now that one of his eyes had swollen shut. And as he spoke, his thick speech suggested a split lip at the least, and more likely some missing teeth.

"My man was murdered," he said. "And…"

But I never heard what he was going to say. The man crouching by Sharpe stood up; he took a couple of steps away, and I could see him a little more clearly. He was my age, perhaps slightly older, clean-shaven, with darkish hair and a heavy jaw. He nodded at his two companions who, with great efficiency and energy, set about kicking Sharpe.

When they had finished, the man in charge moved forward, poked at my friend's body with the toe of his boot, grunted, and then led the others away. As they walked past my hiding place, I moved noiselessly around the pile of barrels to keep out of their sight, all the time keeping them in mine. They did not head back the way I had come, with its guarded doors, but instead made their way to the far corner of the vaults. I was a little disoriented, being underground, but I judged this to be the corner near where Artichoke Hill meets the Ratcliffe Highway above us. It was hard to see exactly what they did, and I dared not move, but I heard the squealing of a hinge and a sudden square of light fell on the floor. It was a trapdoor. There was a clatter as a rope ladder was dropped to the three men and they all climbed up. The ladder was hauled up, with a bang the trapdoor fell shut, and it was dark again.

I waited a few moments and then went over to my friend, kneeling on the cold floor beside him. He was motionless, but jerked when I touched his hand.

"Ben," I said, "it's me, Sam. They've gone."

He groaned.

A terrible thought occurred to me. "I'm sorry about the note, Ben," I said. "About what it said."

He tried to say something and I leaned over him to hear it.

"No note," he said thickly.

"But then why...?" I started to ask, and then recollected myself and scrambled to my feet. "I'll call for help, Ben – hold on just a minute and we'll get help." I ran back through the vaults, the sound of my boots echoing around me. The urgent tattoo must have been heard by the guard, because he met me near the door. I gasped out my story and he yelled up the staircase before returning with me. We carried Ben as best we could between us, trying to jolt him as little as possible, before two other guards arrived with a length of wood on which we could lay him. We each took a corner, manoeuvring our cargo carefully up the stairs, until we reached the office where a wide-eyed, pale-faced Smith was waiting and we could lie Ben on the floor. In the clerk's hand was a bottle of brandy which he handed to me, along with a glass tumbler. I poured a small measure and knelt beside Ben, gently raising his head and dribbling the liquid into his mouth. He winced but swallowed, and then opened his good eye.

"Make sure you note that bottle in the ledger, Smith," he said.

I have never been so happy to hear such a poor jest, and I stayed with my friend, chattering all sorts of nonsense, until the surgeon arrived.

Thomas Neale did as he always does at such times: he brought in a pot of steaming tea. He said nothing, but laid a sympathetic hand on my shoulder as he left. Indeed, there was sympathy aplenty for me when I told my tale back at Great Marlborough Street, but I felt nothing but contempt for myself: what sort of a man cowers around the corner while another – a friend – is beaten in front of him?

Wilson sat opposite me, his notebook open on the table. He was nervous to be quizzing me, I could tell – he kept pulling at his ear, which he does when uneasy – but Neale had suggested that I was in no fit state to make my own clear record of events, and I had to agree with him.

"So you sent Mr Sharpe a message last night," prompted Wilson. "At what time?"

I did a quick calculation in my head. "At about twenty minutes past eleven."

Wilson wrote carefully, then looked up at me. "And can you remember what you wrote in the message? Exactly?"

I tightened my lips, but in truth he was doing what I had taught him: make sure of the details. "'Ben'," I said, "'meet me at the warehouse at nine tomorrow morning – I agree that King might have been murdered'."

Wilson took down my words. "So Mr Sharpe would have been expecting you at nine?"

I nodded. "So I thought. But when he spoke, after the attack, he knew nothing of the message. He was in the vaults to do his morning inspection, not to meet me."

"And anyway," said Wilson, "you said you would meet at the warehouse, not in the vaults. Surely he would wait for you in his office, to save you chasing him around underground."

"So how did his attackers know to find him in the vaults?" I asked.

Wilson looked puzzled, but at my oversight, not at my question. "You said yourself, sir, that Mr Sharpe went there every day at the same time – everyone who worked with him knew that, and a few coins here or there buy that sort of knowledge."

He was right, and Neale had been right not to leave me to my own devices, with my mind so muddled.

"What we don't know," continued Wilson, "is why the three men attacked Mr Sharpe. It was a daring undertaking, breaking into a heavily guarded bonded warehouse. Not something to do on a whim." He paused. "And they had their escape planned. They knew what they were doing."

"I overheard a little of what the one in charge said to Ben," I said. "He told him to leave it alone – that King's death was self-murder. So he knew that Ben suspected otherwise. And he could have known that only from my message. It wasn't the usual lad, not at that time of night. Maybe he sold the message on." I leaned on the table and put my head in my hands. "Dear God, Wilson – it was my fault."

"I don't need an escort," I said irritably to Wilson as he walked beside me. "I am perfectly capable of finding my own way home."

"I know that, sir, but Mr Conant gave very clear orders." Wilson was about to touch my elbow to guide me across Castle Street but dropped his hand when I glared at him. "Anyway, when we sent word to Mrs Plank that you would be returning early, we mentioned that you might be in need of a hearty meal. To get over the shock." He patted his stomach.

There is little more infuriating than trying to be angry with someone so good-natured and guileless, and now I knew that a good feed was in the offing, I understood that Wilson's wish to see me home was as much for his own care as mine. I unbent a touch, and we walked on in companionable silence.

Martha is not given to displays of sentiment but as soon as we opened the gate she came to the door and held her arms open. I stepped into them and her embrace was fierce and determined. She led me into the kitchen, took my coat and pressed me down into a chair. Wilson followed and waited at the door, uncertain. Martha smiled at him.

"I am sure Sam has plenty to tell me, William, but that can wait. Food first."

After a meal at which I found I could only pick, Wilson stood and put on his coat.

"Thank you, Mrs Plank," he said. "That hit the spot. Mr Conant said that Mr Plank is not to come back to work today, but I'll call tomorrow morning as usual, unless you send word."

I considered protesting, but against the massed ranks of magistrate, wife and even junior constable I was helpless. Wilson left and Martha busied herself clearing the table and tidying the pots. I watched her familiar and comforting movements as she went from table to cupboard, from cupboard to range, and I felt the shell cracking as the shame and fear fought their way out. Martha glanced at me, folded her cloth carefully and sat down, silently taking my hand in hers. She waited.

"It was my message, Mar," I said eventually. "My message told them that he, that Ben, suspected it was murder. My message led to him being ambushed and beaten – beaten almost to death."

Martha rubbed my hand gently. "It seems that way, doesn't it?"

One of the many things that I admire – indeed, love – about my wife is her honesty. Others might have blustered to save my feelings, said that it wasn't my fault, but not Martha. If my note had led Ben's attackers to him, it was as well to acknowledge it.

"But, my love," she continued, "how could you have foreseen that? You could not have guessed that the message would fall into the wrong hands."

I shook my head. "I could have guessed it. I should have been more careful."

"Sam, listen to me. Being a constable is about protecting the good and punishing the bad." She stopped and I nodded. "Sometimes you get it wrong: a good person will be punished, or a bad person will escape justice." She stopped again and I nodded again. "But that does not – cannot – mean that you should stop trying. If you let a fear that everyone is bad stop you doing your job, then the good people will suffer." She leaned over and kissed my cheek. "If you start to think that every message lad is in the pay of criminals, then what? You send no messages?"

She was right, of course. I had sent hundreds of messages over the years, and this was the first one about which I had had any doubts. But still, the consequences for poor Ben... Martha narrowed her eyes at me.

"What is it, Sam?" she asked.

I sometimes wonder whether we would do better to dismiss all the judges, lawyers and constables and simply populate the courts with wives; I certainly could hide very little from mine. I spoke almost in a whisper, for what man can bear to tell his wife of his own cowardice? I described to Martha how I had overheard Ben being threatened, how I could see that he was already injured, and how I had held back as he was kicked.

"I should have done something, should have protected him," I said, and hung my head.

Martha's grip on my hand tightened and she spoke with quiet but definite anger in her voice. "Samuel Plank, look at me. I said, look at me." I did so. "This I will not tolerate. You are a brave man – a brave man, a good constable and a loyal friend. But you are not a foolish man, and only a fool would have stepped forward. You were one against three, for a start. And," she held up a hand as I made to talk, "more importantly, for I know you have beaten those odds before, it would have placed Mr Sharpe in even greater danger. If you had shown yourself, in your constable's uniform, those men would have become desperate. And then they would have had to kill you both

– Mr Sharpe for his suspicions, and you because you could identify them. As it is, your friend is alive and you are uninjured, and those three men do not know that you saw the attack and can describe them." I looked at her in astonishment. She shrugged. "Logic and deduction, Sam – logic and deduction."

"And love too, my dear," I said, reaching up to stroke her cheek. "Love too."

CHAPTER TWENTY-ONE

Wilson's heart

WEDNESDAY 28TH FEBRUARY 1827 – MORNING

The next day, as he had promised, Wilson came to call for me. He and Martha engaged in their usual pantomime, where he pretended reluctance to come in and disturb our breakfast, while she pretended despair at all the food that would go to waste if he did not join us. In truth, it was comforting to see them both acting as they always did, although I thought I saw something a little sad in Wilson's face, a little forced about his smile. Martha saw it too; as she was handing me my coat, she whispered, "Bruised heart, I'll wager – tread carefully today."

I'm not one to read signs in nature, but if I were, I would have found plenty of them as Wilson and I walked to

Great Marlborough Street. There was a wintry wind blowing, and its gusts sounded almost mournful as they hurried us down Portland Road. A pair of crows squabbled over something in the gutter, cawing angrily at each other, their black eyes and wings flashing until one abandoned the quarrel. Looking down at the one bird left standing alone, unsure of what to do with its prize, Wilson sighed deeply. I wished fervently that Martha had dealt with this over breakfast.

"Is all well at home?" I asked, thinking – hoping, if I am honest – that he might be preoccupied by something to do with his mother, or the numerous younger siblings for whom he was responsible.

"At home?" he echoed. "Yes, all well, thank you, sir." He sighed again.

"Then what is it, lad?" I asked, taking care to carry on walking and not look at him as I spoke. He said nothing. "If it is something that will affect your work today, it would be as well to admit it."

"We had an argument," he said with a sigh. "Well, not an argument as such – but she said something that worried me."

"She?" I asked.

"Sylvie – Miss Renard."

"Ah." Martha's diagnosis of a bruised heart had been accurate.

"I called on her yesterday evening," he continued. "I have been calling on her regularly; we dine together, the three of us, and then her father goes into his study while Sylvie and I stay at the table, talking."

"I thought that he didn't approve of you – that he wanted a Frenchman for his daughter," I said as we rounded the corner of Charles Street.

"And I thought that I was gradually winning him round with my charm and perseverance," said Wilson, smiling weakly. "But perhaps it was something else."

I waited a minute or two. "Good heavens, lad – spit it out." I stopped where I was; he walked on a few steps and then realised that he was alone and came back to me. I looked around and led him through the gateway into the grounds of the Middlesex Hospital, away from the busy street. There was a stone bench under a tree, and we sat on it. Two young ladies, walking arm-in-arm and giggling, looked over at us with curiosity – Wilson is a handsome fellow, and the uniform flatters us both – but no-one disturbed us. "So," I said.

"So," he said. "I went to call on Sylvie yesterday evening, and she was in a strange mood." I raised an eyebrow. "She seemed distracted, almost as though she wished I was not there."

"Perhaps she did wish that," I said, then chided myself when I saw the crestfallen look on his face. "I mean, perhaps she was not feeling well, or had unfinished chores."

"I tried to amuse her, to entertain her, and I told her about what had happened to you. Not in detail," he went on hurriedly, "I know better than that. But I said that you had seen a man badly beaten, and that it had distressed you." He paused. "She asked me where this had happened, and I said, 'near Custom House'." He stopped again and looked at me. "And then she said, 'Ah yes, the vaults'. But I have gone back over everything in my mind, and I am certain that I never once mentioned the vaults to her."

I thought for a moment. "So she knew about the vaults from someone else?"

He nodded. "And as I recalled our other conversations, things I had said to her and things she had asked me, I started to suspect that perhaps she had been deceiving me." He looked down at his hands, big and strong but now turning over themselves in misery. "Taking advantage of me to learn more about our enquiries."

I took a deep breath and let it out slowly. "I see," I said. I looked around me to give Wilson a moment to himself. "Well," I said, putting my hands on my knees and standing up. "I think the thing to do is to go to the office and write down whatever you can remember of what you told Miss Renard, sweet whisperings aside, so that we can work out what she – and presumably now also her father – knows. You said you spoke only in generalities, so I am sure it's not as bad as you think."

I will admit that I was feeling a great sense of relief, for it had occurred to me that the information that led to Ben's attack could well have come not from my note but from the treacherous Miss Renard. But Wilson looked miserable enough without my adding that, so I kept it to myself.

Wilson got to his feet and we walked back out into the street.

"I daresay," I said as we crossed Oxford Street and I had to drag him out of the way of a wagon and its indignant driver, "that you are at this very minute vowing never to trust a woman again." I looked sideways at him and he gave me a half-smile. "That would be a mistake, you know. Most women – most people – are good, and you will find one worthy of you."

"Like Mrs Plank?" he asked.

I shook my head. "Oh no, not like Mrs Plank. I doubt there is another woman in the whole world like Mrs Plank. But one nearly as good, perhaps, if you are very blessed."

Two tiring hours later, Wilson and I sat back in our chairs. The tea that Tom had brought us had gone cold on the table, and in front of us were several sheets of paper covered in Wilson's deliberate script. Here and there certain words were underlined or circled, where we considered points to be of particular significance. Wilson laced his hands behind his head and closed his eyes.

"You see," I said, and Wilson opened his eyes again, "not as catastrophic as you thought. As far as Miss Renard is concerned, you and I are looking into the possible motives for the possible murder of a customs officer. She knew already that I was interested in Lagrange, as we called on her father to pursue that very matter. And you have not mentioned to her that I met with Lagrange," I looked at Wilson and he shook his head, "nor that you and I have spoken to Bonneville." Wilson gave another shake of the head. "So Miss Renard is aware of our obvious enquiries, but not of the more hidden methods we are employing." I smiled reassuringly at Wilson. "In the future, however, I think it would be prudent of you to talk to Miss Renard of matters other than your work."

He looked even more despondent. "The future?" he said bitterly. "Surely the only thing to do is for me to break with Syl... Miss Renard."

I shrugged and gathered the papers into a neat pile. "I think that is a matter for you – and for her," I said. "She is a beautiful girl – even an old married fellow like me can see that – and lively too. And an excellent cook." My mouth watered at the memory of that delicious stew. "But I would venture that a woman, or indeed a man, who is dishonest at the start of things will rarely become more honest over time. And it is hard to live with distrust in your home; it sours everything it touches." We both sat in silence for a moment. "But enough of this," I said next, standing up and reaching for my coat. "I am hoping to send some news to Mr Sharpe. Do you fancy an excursion to take your mind off things?"

CHAPTER TWENTY-TWO

The river rats

WEDNESDAY 28TH FEBRUARY 1827 –
AFTERNOON

As the coach followed the same route that I had taken a fortnight earlier with Ben Sharpe, my friend was much on my mind. The message delivered to me that morning from the London Hospital had told me that he would live, but that the beating he had received was a severe one – as if I didn't know that myself – and that he seemed confused and could not recall exactly what had happened. Martha had squeezed my hand wordlessly when we read that; the son of one of our neighbours had been kicked in the head by a horse when he was changing its shoe, some fifteen years ago, and although he was a grown man of nearly thirty now, his poor exhausted mother still had to bathe, dress and feed him like an infant.

I tried to put these dark imaginings out of my mind, and occupied myself in pointing out to Wilson the buildings we were passing, hoping to distract him from love-lorn thoughts. He was most impressed by Custom House, and fell respectfully silent as we trundled slowly past the bonded warehouse, caught up once again in the traffic that strangled the narrow roads. Once we had cleared the docks our jarvey turned his horses south towards the river down Gravel Lane, and I found myself back in the stinking, dripping, desperate alleyways of Wapping. I could count the names off on my fingers – Tench Street, Bird Street, Gun Alley – and the bells of St John's church tolled noon as we neared. Wilson looked out of the coach window as we passed the distinctive building, with its striped tower of dark red brick and pale stone.

"The contrast means that it can be seen more clearly through the river mists, so that sailors can tell where they are," I explained, shivering at the thought of those mists, which had crept damply into every corner of my boyhood.

Our coach turned into the high street, and the jarvey pulled it to a halt outside a tall, narrow, pale building, with curved windows on two upper floors overlooking the road and beyond that the foreshore and the river. The river was low, and three of the police's own rowing galleys were hauled up onto the bank and tied to the tall black poles topped with white that served as moorings.

Wilson and I climbed out of the coach and I paid the jarvey. After casting an eye over Wilson's uniform and my own – for it would never do to appear before another constable in shabby dress – I led him up the steep steps into the office.

As in our own police office, the entrance was guarded by an office keeper behind a large counter. Considerably broader in the beam than our Mr Neale in Great Marlborough Street, he nonetheless shared with Tom an ability – no doubt honed over years behind that counter – to see everything he needed in a single glance at a man.

"Constables," he said, leaning forward on two meaty hands. "And how may we mere river rats be of service to you fine city gentlemen?" His smile took the sting out of his question; he was well aware of the nickname we land-based officers had for our watery cousins.

I reached over the counter and shook his hand. "Constable Sam Plank and Constable William Wilson, Great Marlborough Street," I said. "We wanted to speak to your men about smuggling."

"Well, you've come at just the right time," said the office keeper. "Sam Gregory, by the way." He walked out from behind his counter and indicated that we should follow him down the corridor. "Several of the lads are at their midday meal; you can join them and ask all you want," he said over his shoulder. He opened a door to a room at the rear of the building, and we walked into a dining room of sorts. Five men were seated at a long table, and a woman was standing behind one of them, a large pot in the crook of her arm and a ladle in her hand. They all turned to look at us. "Mr Ellis, surveyor. Mr Forster, Mr Anderson and Mr Welling, watermen. Mr Lynds, a blockademan visiting us from Whitstable. And Mrs Gregory," said the office keeper, pointing with each introduction. "Another two plates, my dear – these two gentlemen have come all the way from Piccadilly and are in need of refreshment."

"Piccadilly, eh?" said Ellis, standing to lean across the table and shake my hand. "Great Marlborough Street?"

I took a seat and Mrs Gregory put a dish in front of me, brimming with a thick stew and with a hunk of bread balanced on its edge.

"That's it," I said. "And you're a surveyor here?"

"One of five on river patrol, yes – the other four are out on the water now. I was careful to be back for Mrs Gregory's cooking," said Ellis, smiling, and I could imagine him being popular with his men. "These three are my watermen today."

I nodded a greeting at them; all had the broad shoulders and brawny arms of their trade. "My father was a lighterman," I said. "Worked from Wapping Dock Stairs."

"Not far from here," said Forster, jerking his head downriver. The other two lightermen nodded silently.

"But you fancied life ashore, Mr Plank?" asked Lynds. He was a tall, thin fellow, with dark hair and dark eyes, his skin tanned and leathery from the sun; he looked like the picture of a pirate I had seen in one of Mr Conant's books, which perhaps made him particularly good at his work.

I smiled. "I did. And what brings you to Wapping, Mr Lynds?" I asked.

"We may be miles apart, Mr Plank, but the river joins the blockademen to the river police like a silver rope," he said.

"Very poetical," I remarked.

Ellis barked a laugh. "Ha! You have him exactly, constable – you have him exactly. Joe – Mr Lynds – spends too much time hiding in the marshes and the reeds with only the moon for company; it would bring out the poet in any man, or the lunatic."

Lynds drew himself up in his chair, but decided not to take offence. "To put it more prosaically then, constable, I am here to deliver to Mr Ellis our latest information on a band of smugglers. Tobacco, spirits and salt."

Wilson nudged me under the table.

"Then we are in luck," I said, "for it is about smuggling that we have come."

"Smuggling? In Piccadilly? That would be a rare sight," said Ellis. "Mrs Gregory, I can see from Constable

Wilson's clean plate that your stew meets with his approval. Another serving, if you please."

As Wilson smiled broadly and applied himself to another dish of stew, I explained the outline of our enquiries: the deaths of the artist Rambert and the customs officer King, the beating of my friend, and the trade in French miniatures that seemed to link them all. When I had finished, Ellis was the first to speak.

"An interesting tale, Constable Plank, but – beyond the involvement of Mr King – it seems to have little to do with smuggling, or the customs service," he said. "The import of French paintings is not subject to any duties. If they were coming from China, or the East Indies, yes, but what your French free-traders are interested in is brandy. Spirits of all sorts, tobacco too – but not little paintings of little girls."

The men around the table all nodded in agreement.

"So you are of the opinion that it is a coincidence that one of the victims was a customs officer, and another was beaten nearly to death in a bonded warehouse?" I asked. I did not intend to sound affronted, but a note must have crept into my voice.

"Constable Plank," said Ellis in a gentle tone, "you and I both know that coincidence is much rarer than people might hope. On the contrary, I think there is a connection between all aspects of your story: the artist, the customs officers, the French banker. But that connection is not smuggling. I am sorry."

He was right, of course. It was hard to let go of a theory that had seemed so promising, but foolish to cling to it for that reason alone. I sighed.

The surveyor smiled sympathetically. "But perhaps it is the day for riddles," he said. "Just before you arrived, Mr Lynds was about to tell us about his work. It may interest Mr Wilson, who doubtless shares the thirst of the young for tales of mystery and adventure."

Mrs Gregory walked around the table, gathering our empty dishes and replacing them with tumblers of hot chocolate, and Lynds, leaning forward in his chair and looking at us each in turn to draw us into his circle, began his tale.

"I have been a blockademan in Herne Bay for nearly fifteen years," he began. "Herne Bay is on the north coast of Kent, just east of Whitstable." We all nodded. "We've had a deal of trouble with smugglers, as you can imagine, but the worst were the North Kent Gang – you've heard of them?" Wilson and I shook our heads. "More than fifty of them at one time there were, making camp on Burntwick Island in the Medway, and coming ashore at Stangate Creek or Bishopstone Gap with their contraband." I looked over at Wilson; his eyes were shining at the storybook names. "Early one Easter morning, five or six years ago, we surprised them while they were unloading a boat on the beach at Herne Bay. They fired on us, and when his gun misfired one of our men – Syd Snow, a brave fellow – charged them with his knife. They shot him in the thigh and the shoulder, and we carried him back to our ship. He died the next day." Lynds looked down at his hands. "But thanks to his clear descriptions we got five of them before the judge – including James West, the man in charge. Three of West's so-called comrades gave evidence against him to save their own necks, but their very criminality made their testimony unreliable, and all five were acquitted."

"But..." said Wilson with outrage in his voice.

Lynds held up his hand. "A short-lived triumph, in all senses, lad. West and his two lieutenants were strung up on Penenden Heath less than a year later, and the rest of the gang was transported." Wilson sat back in his seat and exhaled. Lynds smiled at him and continued. "So I've seen plenty of smuggling: gangs and loners, whipper-snappers and square toes, even a few hempen widows taking over their husbands' duties – all of them. But recently something has been puzzling me." He paused and we all waited – I recognised a showman when I saw one. "I first saw it about six months ago." Another pause. "And now I have seen it five times." He looked around the table. "Not unloading a boat from France, but loading it. At dead of night, in Herne Bay." He shook his head in disbelief.

"Loading?" asked Ellis. "You mean the boat comes from France with no cargo, and then someone loads it in Kent and it carries on to London?"

Lynds shrugged. "I doubt it comes all that way with no cargo, but they certainly add to it."

"Are you sure the boats have come from France, and not just from somewhere along our own coast?" I asked.

"When you've been watching the shoreline for as long as I have, you know the regular vessels. And if you get close enough you can hear the Frenchies yammering away. Smell the brandy on their breath, almost." Lynds sat back in his seat and laced his hands behind his head. "So why would a man of Kent need to smuggle anything into London, gentlemen?"

"I have no idea," I said, "but next time it happens, I want to see it for myself."

CHAPTER TWENTY-THREE

Midnight in Herne Bay

MONDAY 5TH MARCH 1827 – MORNING

"Welcome aboard," called Lynds cheerfully as we stepped onto his ship. "I am glad my message reached you in time. After we met last week I thought to check my records, and it seems that there is a pattern to these strange visits: first Monday of the month. To-night." He and I shook hands, but Wilson was reluctant to let go of the railing. He had confided to me as we walked through the dawn light to the docks that he had never been on the river before, and although he pre-tended not to care I could tell he was uneasy. For myself, having spent my early years hopping from lighter to shore and back again I was as comfortable on the river as on land, and indeed I was looking forward to my first river journey for some time.

Lynds took one look at Wilson and nodded sympathetically. "It feels odd for a few minutes, lad, but you'll soon grow used to it. Stand with your legs a bit further apart, like Constable Plank here – that's it – and you'll not lose your balance. As for this old girl," he patted the ship's railing, "she'll see us safe home to Whitstable. Now why don't you two gentlemen settle yourselves down there, and enjoy the sights."

He pointed at a couple of stools at the edge of the deck, and we did as he suggested while he went to speak to the crew in readiness for our departure. After a few minutes we cast off and nosed our way out past Wapping Old Stairs into the middle of the crowded river.

I tapped Wilson on the shoulder. "About here," I said, pointing downwards, "is where they are building the tunnel under the river. Should you like to try it, when it is finished?"

"Not likely," said Wilson. "Much as I'm not keen being on the river, I'm absolutely certain I don't want to be under it."

There was plenty to see, quite apart from the endless traffic on the water. We passed the impressive Grand Surrey Outer Dock and then the river swung south towards Limehouse. The King's Dockyard was next – a veritable hive of activity. On our left were the marshes of the Isle of Dogs, several feet below the level of the river, and the West India Docks, followed soon after on the right by Bugsby's Marshes. I was going to say something about them to Wilson but by then he had nodded off, soothed by the gentle motion of the ship and sheltered from the breeze by the curved side of the ship. I let him sleep; we had had an early start and would need to be vigilant late into the night.

After a passable evening meal at the barracks, we made ourselves as comfortable as we could while we waited. From time to time Lynds would pull out his pocket watch and then go outside to check the winds and weather. Finally, at just gone eleven, he came back in and rubbed his hands together.

"Time to go, gentlemen," he said. "I've checked the tides, and if our fellows keep to form – meeting as near to midnight as possible – we need to set off now if we're to get to Herne Bay in time." He looked around the room at the four of us: Wilson and me, and two other blockademen. We were all dressed in the darkest clothing we could assemble, with black scarves wound up high across our faces and black caps pulled down low, and even black gloves on our hands. "Now remember," continued Lynds, "this is an observation only. We are not planning to engage, but just in case…" He nodded at the two blockade-men and they drew their pistols out of their jackets, checked them and concealed them again. Wilson and I glanced at each other.

At Lynds' direction, we walked away from the barracks in single file: he was at the front followed by one of his men, then came me, then Wilson, and the other armed man brought up the rear. We walked for half an hour or so, going slightly uphill all the while – not enough to tire us, but enough that my knees knew about it. As my eyes adjusted to the dim light, I could see that we were walking on a bluff high above the shore; the ground beneath our feet was sandy and unstable, and with no obvious path to follow we walked through rough, whippy grass that came up almost to our waists.

Lynds knew where he was going, and eventually he stopped and said in a low voice, "Here." As he had instructed back at the barracks, we lay down on our stomachs and crawled forward on our elbows until we found ourselves looking down over the edge onto a large, curved inlet. It was a quiet night with gentle winds. There was a break in the clouds moving slowly across the moon, and "There!" said Lynds. He took a spyglass from his pocket and looked through it before handing it along to me. I raised it to my eye and saw a vessel anchored in the river.

"Can you make out the name?" asked Lynds.

"No," I said, "but perhaps someone with younger eyes..." I passed the spyglass to Wilson.

"V – A – L – E – N," he said. "*Valentine*. And there's a rowing boat heading for it." He paused for a moment. "There are three men in it – no, one man and two lads, one of them quite small." Another short wait. "They're at the *Valentine* now. Someone's leaning over the side, and the small lad – yes, he's only a boy – is handing up a parcel to him. And that's it – they're pushing off now." He handed the spyglass back to Lynds, who looked through it.

"Just the one parcel this time, then," he said, almost to himself. "Wait a minute." He raised himself a little higher on his elbows. "Surely he's not still playing this game." He handed the spyglass to one of his men. "Am I going purblind, or is that Jack Lidgate?" The man checked then nodded wordlessly. Lynds looked again. "And they're heading this way." He thought for a moment. "I think I need a word with Mr Lidgate, gentlemen."

The three blockademen stood up and Wilson and I did likewise. The two armed men took out their pistols and cocked them. We walked in the same order as before, partway down a rough path leading to the cove. When we reached a point with a clear view of the beach, Lynds held up a hand and we stopped. The rowing boat was almost ashore; now I could see that the two doing the rowing were, as Wilson had said, only lads, while sitting on a bench in the bow of the boat was a man of advanced years. When the boat hit the sand, he climbed out and I could see from his bent back and his slow gait that he was a good twenty years older than I. The two lads hopped out after him, and between them they put the oars into the boat and hauled it up the beach, pushing it into some undergrowth. They walked towards the foot of the path on which we were waiting, and I was sure that the others would hear my heart beating. The blockademan next to me shifted his grip on his pistol. Lynds made a motion with his hand and we all stepped back a couple of paces so that we were more concealed. I could hear the footsteps of the three coming closer. The younger lad passed us first, followed by the other one and then Lidgate.

Lynds stepped out. "So it is you, Jack," he said clearly. The three stopped, and Lidgate looked wildly about him. But he quickly saw that they were outnumbered and his eyes settled on Lynds.

"Mr Lynds, isn't it," he said pleasantly. "So here we are again."

Sitting on a low bench with their backs against the wall of the main room of the barracks, the three looked like fish out of water, which I suppose they were. Lynds came out of the back office, a flagon in one hand and a stack of tumblers in the other. He handed round the tumblers to everyone except the younger boy and filled them from the flagon. I sniffed mine; it was an excellent French brandy.

Jack Lidgate threw his down in one swallow and then held out his tumbler again. "That's as good a drop as any I brought in, Mr Lynds," he said.

Lynds poured him another drink and then put the flagon on the table before pulling up a stool and sitting, legs wide, in front of the bench.

"I thought you had retired, Jack," he said. "Seen the error of your ways – or seen too many of your kind swinging on the gibbet. Either way, you're too old for smuggling." Lynds leaned forward. "And you should be ashamed of yourself, leading these two lads astray."

Lidgate drew himself up with indignation. "Smuggling, Mr Lynds – I should think not. What did we bring ashore?" He patted his coat pockets in exaggerated demonstration. "Nothing." He looked around at the rest of us, affronted. "Smuggling, indeed."

"Well if you are so innocent, Jack," said Lynds, leaning back and crossing his arms, "why were you meeting the *Valentine* at dead of night? And why does this lad of yours…"

"My grandson," said Lidgate proudly. "Both my grandsons."

"Why does your grandson look so guilty?" asked Lynds. Lidgate said nothing. Lynds stood up and turned to me. "Ah well, gentlemen, you'd better take them with you; perhaps a few days in Newgate will loosen their tongues."

Lidgate breathed in sharply and the two boys looked at him; they might not know the significance of that particular place, but their grandfather certainly did.

"Ah, did I not say, Jack?" said Lynds. "These two gentlemen are constables from London, sent to find anyone who might know something about the murder of an important customs officer at London Docks. Now you say you weren't smuggling, and that may be the case, but you were certainly up to no good. And unless you can tell us what you were doing, well, we'll have to send you to London to talk to the magistrates so that they can work out whether you were somehow involved in this murder. You and your two lads here."

Lidgate's shoulders dropped; whatever he and his grandsons had been doing, he did not intend to let any of them take the blame for a murder. "I know some of the crew of the *Valentine*," he said. "Frenchies, but none the worse for that. Known them for years. And when I knew they was going to drop anchor in the bay, I asked my lads to row me out. A social call, like."

Lynds sighed deeply. "But you didn't have much to say to your friends, did you, Jack? From what we saw, you stayed sitting while this lad handed up a parcel, and no-one said more than two words to each other."

Lidgate smiled roguishly. "Now why didn't you tell me you saw everything, Mr Lynds? We could have saved ourselves some time." His tone became business-like. "The first Monday of every month, we row out into the bay and hand over a parcel – sometimes two or three – to whatever French ship is anchored there."

"Who gives you the parcels?" asked Lynds, sitting down again.

"They don't come to us direct – we collect them from someone else, and he has them from another hand. Safer that way," said the old man.

"And what's in these parcels?" I asked.

Lidgate shrugged.

"Hah!" said Lynds. "Are you telling me that, old scoundrel that you are, you did not wonder what you were delivering? What was worth so much that it merited such secrecy and so many precautions?"

Lidgate leaned forward, his hands on his knees. "You're right, Mr Lynds – I was curious. And once I did have a look. Jewels, I thought, in a small parcel like that. But it wasn't jewels: it was paintings. Tiny little ones, no bigger than that." He made a circle with his forefinger and thumb. "Some of them were a bit, well, indecent, but nothing to trouble the blockademen." He shook his head. "Seems a lot of trouble to go to, for a frippery like that. Now, a good cask of French brandy, that's worth taking a risk for." He glanced across at the flagon on the table.

Lynds rolled his eyes, but reached over and poured the old smuggler a third drink.

By the time we arrived back at London Docks it was late in the afternoon. We had both slept a little on the ship, but with a stronger wind now whipping up the water beneath us, I think Wilson was relieved to step back onto land. I called over to a jarvey and instructed him to take us to Great Marlborough Street, as Mr Conant had asked us to let him know what we had found as soon as we could. During the journey Wilson was pensive. His notebook was open on his knee – a sure sign that he was thinking about his work.

"What do you make of it all?" I asked. "What would be the purpose of loading – of clandestinely loading – a parcel of miniature paintings onto a vessel in Herne Bay, for them to be taken to London?"

"As an alternative to the mail coach?" suggested Wilson.

"Perhaps – but the river route would be slower and less predictable, with the tides, and it seems an unnecessarily risky way to send a valuable package. There must be some reason for them wanting it to arrive on that ship. A ship from France." I paused to allow Wilson to come up with the answer first.

He turned to me. "To make it look as though the paintings had come all the way from France with the rest of the cargo. To make the paintings seem French." I raised an eyebrow. "So that buyers will pay more for them."

I smiled at him.

When the coach stopped outside Great Marlborough Street, I paid the jarvey and then told Wilson to wait for me outside the door leading to the stairs up to Mr Conant's rooms. Wilson looked surprised, but I left him crouching down to put a shine on his boots with the cuff of his coat. Thomas Neale was just readying himself to go home and confirmed that the magistrate was in residence upstairs. I cast an eye over Wilson; he looked tidy enough. He and I climbed the stairs to the door of Mr Conant's dining room and I knocked.

"Come," called the magistrate, and I led Wilson into the room. He tried to stay near the door, but I turned and ushered him forward with me. Mr Conant was – as so often – working on papers at the table, and he held up a hand in welcome, the other carefully marking his place. "A minute, if you please, gentlemen – I am finally reaching the end of this tedious tale. Be seated."

There were two armchairs facing the fireplace and I pointed to one of the dining chairs, but Wilson shook his head. He had once confessed to Martha that he felt untidy in a chair, with his great long legs, and preferred to stand if neatness was required, and so I took one of the armchairs and Wilson stood behind me. A few minutes later Conant laid down his spectacles on the pile of papers and walked over to the sideboard, picking up a decanter.

"A drink, gentlemen?" he asked. Ordinarily I would have accepted, but I guessed that Wilson, discomfited by chairs, would be terrified by a delicate glass, and so I shook my head. Conant poured himself a generous measure and came to sit in the armchair across from me. He raised his glass in salute and drank gratefully.

"As you know, sir," I said, "we have been to Herne Bay in Kent. We went in search of information about smuggling but came away with something much more useful, concerning our interest in the trade in French miniatures." Conant settled himself into his chair; he was an excellent listener. "And Constable Wilson has worked out what is going on."

"Indeed," said Conant, looking up at Wilson with an encouraging smile. "I am delighted to hear it."

Wilson cleared his throat. "Last night we watched a ship at anchor in Herne Bay – a French ship called the *Valentine*, bound for London. A rowing boat went up to it and delivered a parcel. When we spoke to the men in the rowing boat, they said that the parcel contained miniature paintings." He stopped.

"So we wondered why..." I prompted.

"So we wondered why anyone would go to all that trouble to make sure that the miniature paintings arrived on a ship from France," continued Wilson in a rush.

"Quite," said Conant, nodding. "There is no duty payable on them, or on any of the materials used in their creation, so why be secretive about their shipment?"

"But what if people want to think that the miniatures have come from France? What if that makes them more valuable?" Wilson said.

The magistrate sipped his drink again. "Winstanley – my wife's cousin, you remember?" I nodded. "Well, he was certainly keen that I should know that his collection was French – the last valuables sold by a desperate family with good blood but no money. So yes," he nodded and smiled up at Wilson, "that could certainly explain it. You did well to think of it."

Wilson turned red but looked very pleased.

"And now, gentlemen, you must go home for one of Mrs Plank's excellent meals." The magistrate reached into his pocket and handed me a few coins. "By coach, I think, after your exertions."

"That was a kindness, Sam," said Martha that night as we readied ourselves for bed. "I could have done without hearing the story three times over dinner, but I have rarely seen William so talkative." She stood to shake her nightgown over her head, and I marvelled that her shape had changed so little since the night she became my wife and I saw it for the first time. I held up the covers and she slipped into bed and curled into the crook of my arm.

"To be honest, he has come along so well recently that I think he might have come to the same conclusion himself," I said. "He is mortified that Miss Renard fooled him, but it has certainly made him a better constable: he listens more and trusts less."

"But still, Sam," said my wife, reaching up to stroke my cheek, "it was good of you to let him tell Mr Conant."

"What we need now is proof that buyers are being lied to about the provenance of the paintings…" I tailed off as Martha turned to me and kissed me. Kindness, it turns out, is much underestimated as the way to a woman's heart.

CHAPTER TWENTY-FOUR

Familiar faces

FRIDAY 9TH MARCH 1827

Three days later, Wilson and I once again picked our way through the debris and filth filling the narrow gutters lining the alleyway leading to Bonneville's "petit studio". Wilson had protested at being squeezed into his dandy's outfit again, but his protests were half-hearted: like me, he sensed that we were closing in on what Bonneville was really doing, and with that in mind he could put up with a little discomfort. Nonetheless, he kept pulling at his tall collar and muttering darkly about vanity. I let him: a whining, complaining demeanour suited his character today.

The same grubby maid opened the green door and led us up the same stairs, but this time Bonneville was much more unctuous in his welcome; our prompt and generous payment after our last meeting had obviously convinced him of our value. He scurried over as soon as we appeared in his doorway and waved us into his room, almost bowing as we passed him.

"Lord Nameless," he said, a weasely smile on his lips, "a great pleasure – a great pleasure – to see you again. Your communication the week before last distressed me, at the notion that my little delay was causing you inconvenience."

"Hmmph," grunted Wilson, walking across the room and depositing himself into the only comfortable chair.

"But your timing was most fortuitous," continued Bonneville, his hands clasped in front of him, "as only hours after I received your letter, I heard that your shipment was en route."

Our curt note to Bonneville, suggesting that Lord Nameless was losing patience and might seek to take his business elsewhere, had had the desired effect. The previous evening a lad had come to the front office of Great Marlborough Street with a message addressed to Lord Nameless at his gambling club, one of the dozen or more such establishments located in the back streets of St James. This was the address we had given Bonneville when we first met him, reasoning that it would bolster the lord's reputation as a profligate young fool, and a quick word with the clerk at the club soon convinced him that conniving with us and sending on any messages thus addressed would be to his advantage.

"Hmmph," said Wilson again, inspecting the finger-nails of one hand. Thanks to Martha's ministrations that morning, they were the cleanest and neatest I had ever seen them. "So you have something for me?"

"Indeed I do, indeed I do, just as promised in my message," said the art tutor. He moved a small side table next to Wilson's chair and then retrieved a tray, covered in a dark red cloth, from another table and laid it in front of Wilson. "May I?" he said. Wilson gave a curt nod, and with a flourish Bonneville removed the cloth from the tray. "No hills or horses, as you can see, my lord," he said.

Displayed on the tray were five miniature paintings. Two were of individual women, half-portraits in small oval frames, while the other three were slightly larger, rectangular group compositions. Wilson reached for-wardly languidly, as though bored by the whole business, and picked up one of the individual paintings before handing it wordlessly to me. For his own inspection, he selected one of the group portraits. I looked down at the miniature in my hand. It showed a young woman – aged perhaps eighteen – draped in a loose golden garment of vaguely classical design. Around her head, catching up her hair, was a piece of red ribbon. A similar ribbon was used to fasten her garment over her shoulder, but it was unequal to the task and her robe had slipped, displaying her breasts. Her shy smile, her face half-turned away, hinted that she was unaware of her naked state. Wilson held his hand up without looking at me and we exchanged portraits. In the one I was now holding, three naked women danced in a garden, holding hands and entirely absorbed by each other, seemingly oblivious to the artist.

Wilson held the woman in the golden robe for a moment, and then replaced her on the tray. "Very fine, Bonneville, very fine," he said. "I will take them."

As we had practised, I bent to whisper into his ear.

"Although, given the price you have quoted, I would need... assurances," Wilson glanced up at me and I nodded, "assurances that these are French. They are pretty pieces, to be sure, but you do charge rather a generous premium," another glance from him, another nod from me, "for their exoticism."

"My dear sir," said Bonneville, mock effrontery in his tone, "you have my personal assurance of this. My word." He placed a hand on his heart for emphasis. Wilson said nothing, but made as though to stand. "Although," said the Frenchman hurriedly, "for my own records I did ask the captain of the ship for a receipt." He went over to a cabinet and opened a small cupboard door. "And he gave me this." He handed Wilson a piece of paper, and Wilson passed it on to me without looking at it.

I knew what it was immediately: it was an identical form to the ones I had found in King's room. All the spaces were completed, showing that a ship called the *Val-*

entine had docked in London on 6th March last and unloaded a cargo of brandy and wine. I had no doubt that these details would be correct, as would the name of the ship's captain, Pierre Clément, and his signature: they would not be so foolish as to fabricate something that could be verified at Custom House. The signatures of the two customs officers were, unsurprisingly, illegible, and at the foot of the document, nice and clear this one, was the signature of the clerk responsible for transcribing it into the ledger – J Morgan. Who had been dead some months by the time the *Valentine* made her way into the docks.

I looked up at Bonneville. "And this is the ship on which these paintings were brought to London? The *Valentine?*" I saw Wilson stiffen slightly at the mention of the familiar name, but he quickly mastered himself and Bonneville noticed nothing.

The art tutor nodded. "The captain himself gave them to me, and he had them from our agent in France. Lagrange mentioned this arrangement?" It was my turn to nod. "And when the capitaine – captain – went to Custom House to complete his registration, he asked for a second copy of the docket, which you see." Bonneville held out his hand for the paper, but I folded it and put it in my pocket. He smiled nervously and, to busy his hands, started wrapping the five miniatures in the red cloth and then handed the bundle to me.

"All in order?" asked Wilson, yawning widely.

"Yes, my lord," I said.

Wilson stood and walked to the door, where he waited until Bonneville hurried over and opened it for him.

"If you decide to expand your collection further, my lord, you have only to say the word," said the art dealer, bowing as we left his room.

Back out in the street, Wilson strode in front of me until we had left the studio in Bateman's Buildings far behind us and could walk as equals once more. My mind was on our conversation with Bonneville, so it was with some surprise that I realised that we were walking towards Great Marlborough Street, even though our uniforms were both back at my house, airing in the yard. As I turned on my heel to head home, Wilson seemed reluctant, and I have rarely known him reluctant to go to my house at meal times.

"But sir," he said, indicating the red parcel under my arm, "surely we should deal with those at the office." He coloured slightly. "We cannot examine them in front of Mrs Plank," he said quietly, looking over his shoulder as though he expected to find Martha standing there.

"Your concern for Mrs Plank is admirable," I said, trying to keep the chuckle out of my voice, "but I think you will find that she is more familiar with the female form than either of us."

After we had both taken off our costumes, and all three of us had enjoyed a fine meal, Martha cleared the table and handed me the package of paintings that I had left unopened on the dresser. Wilson moved to sit beside me and Martha stood behind us. I put the package carefully on the table and unfolded it, taking out the five miniatures one by one and setting them down. There were the two Wilson and I had inspected at Bonneville's studio, and the three others. We all looked silently at them. After a moment, Martha leaned forward and picked up the portrait of the girl in the golden gown.

"It is finely done," she observed, "although not as lovely as Elizabeth."

"I suspect that it is a different artist," I said. "If, as we think, these are being painted to order, Rambert was already dead when Wilson – or rather, Lord Nameless – requested them."

Wilson, reassured by Martha's calm assessment of the paintings, reached out for the other solo portrait. He turned it over and peered closely at the back of the frame, then looked at me with a broad smile.

"Here," he said, pointing to a mark on the frame. "Do you remember that sale we went to in the Strand? The one where Bonneville bought those miniature frames?" I nodded. "Well, when the porter was showing me the frames before he packed them up, I used my penknife to make a mark in the back of one of them – a tiny cross. And here it is." He handed me the frame, and indeed there it was: Wilson's mark scratched into the metal.

"So this portrait – supposedly brought over from some aristocratic collection in France – has mysteriously found itself in a frame bought, what, a couple of weeks ago in the Strand," I said. "Well done, lad – well done."

I handed the frame back to Wilson and he replaced it on the cloth and picked up one of the group portraits. He had gazed at it for only a moment when he said in a ragged tone, "Dear God!" I looked at him and he was pale, both hands clutching the small rectangular frame.

"What is it, William? Are you unwell?" asked Martha, pulling out the chair next to him and sitting in it to peer into his face.

He shook his head wordlessly and stared at the portrait. I leaned over to look at it.

"The girl on the left," he whispered. "It must be her."

The painting was of three young ladies preparing themselves for an outing – a ball, I supposed, from the gowns hanging in readiness. The three were, of course, in a state of considerable undress; the one on the left had her foot up on a chair as she unrolled a stocking up her leg, and she looked over her shoulder out of the frame.

Her dark eyes and the deep, rich red of her curling hair were unmistakable. Martha looked at me.

"Miss Renard," I said.

"Oh, William," said Martha. "I am sorry." She held out her hand. "Here: let me have that – there is no need to distress yourself further." William passed her the painting and she looked down at it. And gasped. I wondered whether I had overestimated her worldliness after all and she was shocked by the composition.

"Sam," she said slowly. "The girl in the centre. The one stepping out of her bath. I know her." My wife looked up at me with tears bright in her eyes. "It is Jane Caldwell. She is one of our girls at the school."

CHAPTER TWENTY-FIVE

A bad apple at Custom House

MONDAY 12TH MARCH 1827

I had just reached the end of Poland Street when a message lad caught hold of my sleeve.

"Beg pardon, Constable Plank, sir," he said, "but Mr Neale asks if you would come back to the office, sir."

I pulled my watch out of my pocket; with a bit of luck, I could attend to this and still reach home in time for dinner. I sent Wilson on ahead to warn Martha while I turned back towards Great Marlborough Street. The lad trotted alongside me – he knew that soft-hearted Tom would give him a coin and something to eat when he returned with his quarry.

"Sorry to call you back, Sam," said the office-keeper when we went into the front office. "Feet," he said, pointing at the message lad's boots, which were indeed filthy. The boy wiped them energetically on the mat but it served only to create a dust-storm around him. "Wait outside, and I'll bring you something in a moment," said Tom. The lad saluted with a grin and stomped down the steps. Tom turned to me. "There's a fellow waiting to see you in the back office. I tried to tell him to come back tomorrow, but he said it was difficult for him to get here, and that it had to be you. Skinny as you like – makes Thin Billy look well covered."

The man waiting in the back office leapt to his feet as I walked in, and I recognised the clerk from Custom House.

"Owen Avery, Clerk of the Second Class," I said, shaking his hand.

"I am sorry to recall you from your dinner, constable, but having journeyed here today, making sure all the way that no-one was following me, I could not face repeating it tomorrow." The poor man looked as nervous as a kitten.

"Following you, Mr Avery?" I said, taking a seat and indicating that he should do the same. "Why should anyone be following you?"

The clerk sat and then leaned towards me. "We have found how those signed receipts fell into the wrong hands. It was," he swallowed, "a Custom House junior clerk. One of our own men. And if there is one bad apple," he looked over his shoulder and then back at me and dropped his voice, "there may be more." He shook his head sadly. "That it should come to this, constable. It has quite destroyed my faith in the sanctity of the Long Room."

This is a repercussion of dishonesty that few consider: it takes good, decent people and makes them doubt and mistrust, and all of us are then the poorer for it. The clerk did right to compare it to a rottenness. Nonetheless, I sought to reassure him.

"How many men work in the Long Room, Mr Avery?" I asked.

"Nearly two thousand, taking into account officers, clerks, tide-waiters and so on. Why do you ask?"

"You are a man of numbers, sir," I said. "And with one bad man among two thousand, the odds are surely in favour of honesty and diligence." I smiled. "Now, what was it you came to tell me? About this junior clerk?"

"But this man no longer works in Custom House? This William Smith?" asked Wilson.

"No," I confirmed. "After Smith had been dismissed for his slovenly attitude – almost a hanging offence in the Long Room, according to Mr Avery – another junior clerk came forward to confess that he had seen Smith putting some papers into his satchel at about the time the signed receipts went missing, just after Mr Morgan died. This other junior clerk had challenged Smith, who intimated that he had some very short-tempered friends who would not be happy with any interference, and so the junior clerk turned a blind eye."

Martha put our plates on the table and took her own seat. "So Mr Morgan signed the receipts and then died, and the receipts were stolen by Mr Smith and passed on – or perhaps sold – to Mr King, who completed them with genuine information and gave them to Mr Bonneville to convince his buyers that their paintings had been brought in from France." She looked at me and I nodded. "But who is in charge? Who told Mr Smith to steal the receipts?"

"That, my love, is what we have to consider now," I said, tearing a piece of bread and dipping it into my gravy.

"Well, I suppose you shall have to find Mr Smith and ask him," she said.

"That is exactly what I was hoping you would suggest," I said. "I have a fair idea where this Smith is right now, and so Wilson and I will have to go out after dinner."

Martha opened her mouth to object, but she knew she had been cornered. Wilson bent his head lower over his plate, and I could see his shoulders shaking as he tried not to laugh.

Familiar though it is, Piccadilly after dark is a different place. At night the streets belong to the taverns and the trollops rather than the merchants and the magistrates. Wilson and I strode into Regent Street, passing first our usual turning into Great Marlborough Street and then the grand residences that lined this finest of streets. We followed the curve of the road into the Quadrant, the expensive shops dark and the pillared arcade outside them now the shadowy province of the ladybirds and their customers. On Piccadilly, in contrast, the impressive bulk of Burlington House was ablaze with lights, the carriages thronging its courtyard suggesting a glamorous evening entertainment.

By the time we arrived at Arlington Street, the clock of St James on Piccadilly had just struck a quarter to ten. Tom Neale's encyclopaedic knowledge of London's seamier side had once again proved invaluable, and from him I knew that the majority of the gambling clubs in St James started their serious business at about ten at night, including the one where William Smith now worked. This was no White's or Brook's; this gambling hell had no pretensions to be a gentlemen's club, but existed purely to provide young men of good means and bad morals with every opportunity to lose their money at vingt-et-un or hazard or on the roulette wheel. As we waited in the shadows, several men turned into the street and went into the hell through the workers' door tucked in along-side the main entrance. My plan was to allow them all to arrive and then demand to see the director of the place and ask him to point out our man, but just as the hour was striking, a familiar young man with curling fair hair ran up the street.

"Mr Smith," I called out before I could stop myself.

Wilson looked at me with surprise. "How do you know that it is he?" he asked.

The man had stopped and was looking across at me. I walked towards him. "Constable Sam Plank," I said.

"Constable?" The man looked uneasily about him. "Do I know you, sir?"

"From Pennington Street," I explained. "We met the day Mr Sharpe was attacked."

"Ah, Pennington Street," he replied with relief. "Then I am not the Mr Smith you seek, constable. You mean my brother, Frederick. I am William. We are all but identical, as you can see." He smiled winningly; I remembered that his brother too had an angelic face. "And now, sir, if you will excuse me, I am late and my pay will be docked."

He turned to go and I laid a hand on his arm. "You are mistaken, sir. Although I do know your brother, you are very much the Mr Smith whom I wish to see tonight."

The director of the club was none too pleased to see one of his puffs arriving in the company of two constables, and quickly ushered all three of us into the cupboard he grandly called his office. He tried to stay himself, but I held the door open to indicate that he should leave and closed it firmly after him. Smith appropriated the most comfortable chair in the room, the director's I should imagine, and Wilson moved towards him but I gave a small shake of my head; if a man feels he has won a skirmish, he can become careless about the war. I perched on the only other chair, while Wilson stood with his back to the closed door. Above us we could hear bursts of masculine laughter.

"Mr Smith," I said, taking out my notebook and opening it ostentatiously, "I understand that you were once in the employ of Custom House, working as a junior clerk in the Long Room."

"What of it?" replied Smith. I heard a creak as Wilson took a step towards us, and Smith thought better of it. "That's right, yes," he said hurriedly. Wilson retreated.

"And why did you leave what must have been a good position, with more regular working hours?" I asked.

"I've never been much good with regular, with rules and regulations," said Smith. "Not like Frederick – he's the one for ledgers and records, for keeping everything just so. I prefer a more free and easy way of working." We both looked up to the ceiling at another peal of raucous laughter. "Like here."

"You were simply not suited to the work, then," I said, making a note in my book and waiting a few moments. "No other reason?" I like to give a man time to come clean – it sits well with the judge, does confession, even at a late stage.

"No other reason, no," said Smith.

"Have you seen this paper before?" I reached into my pocket and took out one of the blank, signed receipts that I had found in King's room, unfolded it and placed it on the tiny desk between us.

"Ah," he said.

"Now, Mr Smith," I said, "are you going to insult my intelligence, and your own, by continuing with this pretence – for pretence it is – that your only sin at Custom House was not to fit in with their way of working?" I tapped my open notebook. "We have all the confirmation we need from other clerks in the Long Room to take this matter before the magistrates, and, you can be sure, those particular gentlemen will take an extremely dim view of the forging of official customs documents." I retrieved the receipt from the desk, folded it and put it carefully into my pocket. "Or are you going to tell us who is calling the tune?"

If a man is willing to cheat one person he will be willing to cheat everyone, and William Smith, seeing a way to save his own skin, had no qualms about betraying his conspirators. In fact, for a man with loyalty only to himself, he had found himself the ideal position in life. His master at the gambling hell required him to tempt those who were losing money to stake more, by convincing them that their luck was about to turn. And his master elsewhere paid him handsomely to pass on the names of wealthy young gentlemen who might be interested in, as Smith put it with a wink, "purchasing the sort of paintings best kept in private collections for personal enjoyment".

"I see," I said. "And the name of this master?"

Smith shook his head.

"And is this all he asks of you, the names of potential customers?" I said. I patted the pocket that contained the forged Custom House receipt. "Come now, Mr Smith. We know that you stole the receipts, and we also know where they ended up. Was it you who filled in the forged details, or did you sell on the documents as blanks?"

Smith slumped in his seat. "I sold them as blanks – if they have been completed since then, that is not down to me."

"And so, Mr Smith, I ask you again: the name of this master, if you please."

"I cannot," said the young man earnestly. "Anyway, I have never met him: we communicate by message only."

"Very well, Mr Smith," I said, rising from my chair. "I hope that, whoever he is, he appreciates the service you render him as you climb the scaffold for his crimes of forgery. I doubt he would do the same for you."

The puff chewed his lip. "Renard," he said eventually. "At a banking house in Craven Street."

CHAPTER TWENTY-SIX

A conspiracy of clerks

WEDNESDAY 14TH MARCH 1827

"**M**r Freame is with a client, but he says you're to wait here by the fire and I'm to bring you some tea to warm you," said the young clerk, standing aside to let me walk into the parlour at the rear of the banking hall. The banker's note, saying that he had some information about Renard, had arrived at Great Marlborough Street first thing that morning, and with my own news to impart to him, the timing could not have been better.

"Thank you," I said. "Stevenson, isn't it?" The clerk nodded. "So Mr Freame still has you carrying the tea-tray, then."

The clerk smiled; he and I could both remember a couple of years earlier, when Freame had taken him on, a gangling lad, and had waited patiently through spilled tea, cracked cups and – no doubt – smudged ledgers for the young man to learn his trade.

"Only for his most valued visitors, sir," he said.

"Which you most assuredly are, my dear constable," said Edward Freame, appearing in the doorway. Stevenson bowed and withdrew. I stood and the banker and I shook hands and then settled ourselves into the two armchairs. We talked of the foul weather and our fair wives before Stevenson returned with the tea and a plate of biscuits. Freame patted his stomach and eyed up the biscuits.

"I should not, Sam, but if you were to, well, it would be impolite of me to leave you to eat alone..." he said with a half-smile. We each took a biscuit and sat back in our chairs. "It is good of you to come so promptly. Is young Wilson not with you? I thought he had an interest in this matter."

"Indeed he does," I said, "and more of an interest than you might imagine, which I shall explain in due course. But he has gone with Martha today, to your school, to speak to one of the girls there. Jane Caldwell."

Freame stood, dusting the biscuit crumbs from his front, and retrieved a leather-bound book from his shelf. "Caldwell, Caldwell," he said, turning its pages. "Ah, yes,

Jane – here we are." He sat down and read aloud the entry. "Mother in service – unmarried. Father unknown, of course. Jane has been attending the school since last autumn. Aged twelve on admission, now thirteen. Literate." He ran his finger along the page. "Commendations for fine needlework and neat dress. One bad mark for talking in chapel." He looked up at me, suddenly serious. "But if a constable has gone to see her, I fear that talking in chapel is not the end of it."

"Here." I reached into my pocket and took out the miniature that had so upset Wilson and Martha the previous evening, wrapped in a handkerchief. I handed it to Freame, who unwrapped it, raised an eyebrow and then looked more closely.

"Ah," he said. "And which one is Jane?"

"The one in the middle," I said. "And the red-haired one on the left – that is Miss Sylvie Renard. The daughter of Pascal Renard." This time both of Freame's eyebrows shot up. "And Constable Wilson's sweetheart."

Freame handed the miniature back to me and I told him all that we had learned so far, about Bonneville and Lagrange, about the forged documents supposedly showing that the paintings had been brought in from France, about our adventures in Kent, and about the frames bought here in London, with Renard involved at seemingly every turn. Freame listened carefully, taking occasional sips of his tea and letting his hand stray to the biscuits. When I had finished, he sighed deeply.

"Do you think that Renard knows?" he asked.

"About his daughter?" I shook my head. "Let us hope not."

"No, not about that," said Freame. "About Bonneville and Lagrange lying to their customers – selling them new English paintings while charging them for old French ones."

"Although of course the two men were offering slightly different services," I said. "Lagrange was claiming to find existing paintings in France, while Bonneville led his customers to believe that he was commissioning artists in France to paint to order."

Freame shrugged. "They were both lying about what they were selling, and charging a handsome premium for it. It pains me, as a fellow banker, to say it, but it seems to me that Renard must have known that deception was involved. After all, he paid this lad in the gambling hell – Smith – to pass on the names of possible gulls."

"I tend to agree with you," I said. "When a man's name comes up again and again, it cannot be ignored. But if we are to determine that Renard was indeed a party to the deception – and certainly if we are to convince a magistrate of it – we will need to find out whether he had a motive."

Freame smiled at me; he knew my fondness for exploring why a man commits a crime and not just knowing that he has done so.

"Perhaps it was simply for money," I said, "for his portion of the takings. The banking house seemed to be thriving, and Craven Street is becoming a popular part of town, but then bankers can be adept at hiding the true state of their finances."

"Ah, well, I may be able to shed some light on Renard's interests, which was the reason for the note I sent you," said Freame. "But it is not my story to tell."

Just then there was a knock on the parlour door and Stevenson looked into the room.

"More tea, Mr Freame?" he asked.

The banker beamed at him. "Stevenson, your ability to show up exactly when you are needed is uncanny, and will serve you particularly well in banking. Come in, come in."

"I begin to think it impossible for a man in London to keep a single secret to himself," said Mr Conant as he removed his spectacles, put them on top of the pile of papers at his elbow, and rubbed the bridge of his nose. "Or at least any poor fellow who falls under your gaze." He stood and straightened himself, his hands at the small of his back. "The clerk, you say?"

"Yes: Mr Freame's clerk Stevenson knows the junior clerk at Renard's banking house."

"And it is this clerk who suggests that his master – Monsieur Renard – has these... sympathies," asked the magistrate.

I nodded. Conant sat in one of the chairs and I took the other.

"The clerk says that there are regular meetings in Mr Renard's rooms above the banking hall – 'earnest discussions', Stevenson called them. And there is something a little more complicated than that," I added.

"More complicated than a Frenchman in our midst with revolutionary sympathies?" asked the magistrate with some surprise.

"Constable Wilson has become rather entangled in the situation. Unintentionally, of course," I said quickly, "and nothing to do with revolution. More to do with the heart."

"Ah, the heart," said the magistrate. "As you say, even more complicated than mere revolution. Poor fellow."

"He formed something of an attachment to Renard's daughter. The attachment is at an end now; Wilson realised that the young lady was using him to keep track of our interest, and then she appeared in one of the paintings sold to us, in an immodest pose," I explained.

"Ah," said Conant again. "And how is Constable Wilson?"

"Mortified," I said. "Although Mrs Plank assures me that his heart is not broken – merely bruised, along with his pride."

"I'm glad to hear it," said the magistrate. "But while he was under Miss Renard's spell, did he tell her anything of concern?"

I took a deep breath. "I fear that he may have led her father's men to Mr Sharpe."

Conant looked at me. "Then I am very sorry for it, Sam." He shook his head. "It is a lesson hard learnt for Constable Wilson. But it is learnt?"

"Oh yes," I said. "Very well learnt."

We sat in silence for a minute or two; for my part, I thought of Ben Sharpe. His wife had sent me a note to say that although his injuries were healing he would never walk again, and for such an active man, that would be a torture.

"Renard is not alone, you know," said Conant eventually. "Think of Peterloo, and the Cato Street conspirators, only a few years ago. There are apparently some here in London – Frenchmen mostly, but some Englishmen too – who look back to 1789 and to how France changed under Boney, and wish that for us. The government is concerned enough about it, I am told, to task spies with identifying those who might foment discontent."

"A revolution, you mean?" I asked.

"An uprising of the people to rid us of the King and his court and lead to a more equitable society – as they see it," he replied.

I laughed. "Aye, as they see it – that's the thing, isn't it? As I recall, Boney was quite keen on building up his own fortune and garnishing his own family with land and titles."

The magistrate nodded. "Indeed: égalité is often a pre-scription for others, and rarely a medicine for oneself."

"But you think that Renard may be supporting such a cause?"

Conant considered. "Perhaps. It would certainly ex-plain why he needs money: revolution is not cheap."

"And," I said slowly, a thought coming to me, "it would particularly please him to make fools of people like Lord Winstanley, whose privilege such a man would despise." I stopped as Conant leapt to his feet.

"Winstanley!" he said. "Dear heavens, I am to dine with him tonight – it had slipped my mind." He went to the door and yelled down the stairs for his footman.

I stood to go. "Mr Conant, sir," I said as the magistrate shrugged off his coat and started to undo his cravat, "when you see Lord Winstanley this evening, will you tell him what we have learned? About the origin of the paint-ings he has bought from Bonneville?"

Conant's footman Thin Billy came into the room, an evening coat over his arm. The magistrate paused in front of his looking glass, and caught my eye in the reflection.

"Winstanley is a prize buffoon – we are agreed on that," he said. "Anyone who has met the man agrees on that, is that not so, Williams?" The footman handed the magistrate a clean cravat but wisely said nothing. "It would be just like Winstanley to go running to Bonneville demanding his money back, and all would be revealed. But on the other hand I cannot let him blunder on in complete ignorance. So I will tell him, Sam," he said, holding out his hand for his evening coat, "but I will also caution him not to take any action on his own, and will assure him that we are acting in his best interests. But we must act quickly, before more rich men contribute unknowingly to the revolutionary cause."

CHAPTER TWENTY-SEVEN

Less than spotless beginnings

FRIDAY 16TH MARCH 1827

I walked into the back office of Great Marlborough Street and was surprised to see James Harmer sitting there.

"Constable Plank," he said, standing to shake my hand. "You will forgive me for coming into your inner sanctum; I will be on my feet later," he jerked his head towards the courthouse next door, "and I cannot bear the company of my fellow lawyers as we wait to be called. One of them in particular is an odious man, but professional courtesy means that, if I see him, I have to converse with him – and so I hide myself away in here. Mr Neale was kind enough to furnish me with a cup of tea and yesterday's newspaper."

The lawyer sat down again and I took off my coat and sat opposite him.

"As you are here, Mr Harmer," I said, "I would be grateful for your view on something that is puzzling me."

Harmer pushed away the newspaper and sat back. "I have found in the past, constable, that things that puzzle you are always worth pondering. Fire away."

"Constable Wilson and I have been looking at the trade in French miniature paintings, as you know." The lawyer nodded. "And we have discovered that miniatures are being painted here in England and then sold to people as French works, either painted to order or bought from French noble families, and always sold at a premium for being French."

"Rarity," said the lawyer, nodding. "Exoticism."

"I daresay," I said. "But the willingness of people to pay more for a painting of a French nude than one of an English nude is not what puzzles me." Harmer raised his eyebrows but said nothing. "One buyer who has been duped is a cousin of Mr Conant's late wife, and the other evening Mr Conant told him of the deception and of our plans to unmask the men behind it. But the fellow said that he wants nothing to do with it, that he does not want to be involved in any way."

"Of course not," said Harmer. "He is a wealthy man, I take it?" I nodded. "We must remember that the wealthy man values things differently to the rest of us. If this wife's cousin does pursue the man who has deceived him, the most he can hope for is to reclaim his money – and to a rich man, such a sum will be of little consequence. What will matter much more to him is his reputation, and having his name read out in court will pain him greatly. It will broadcast his foolishness to the world."

"So he will simply keep the paintings and enjoy them as best he can?" I asked.

The lawyer laughed. "Constable Plank, he is far from the first man to find himself in possession of paintings that are not what he thought. No, this is a well-trodden path, I am afraid. You say that the paintings are of a private nature, nudes and the like?" I nodded. "Well, in that case he will have plenty of friends who will covet them and will be willing to buy them from him; he may even tell them the truth about their criminal origins, or a version of it, as a little intrigue may increase their appeal. Or he may choose to keep the miniatures in the family for a generation or two, by which time they will have acquired their own respectability and no-one will question their pedigree. The fine homes of England, I am afraid, are stuffed with paintings and sculptures whose beginnings are less than spotless."

There was a light knock at the door and the office-keeper appeared. "You are wanted next door, Mr Harmer, sir," he said.

Harmer stood and straightened his coat. "I hope that has helped, constable," he said as he followed Tom out of the room. "Those who buy items in secrecy bind themselves by the same secrecy, you see. If they have bought what they should not, they have no recourse to the law. And those who sell to them know it."

The leaping fish dish

TUESDAY 20TH MARCH 1827

"Are you sure I should not come with you?" asked Wilson.

"Certain," I replied, hanging my blue constable's coat on the hook and putting on my plain one instead. "All I am going to do is present Bonneville with your next order. A gentleman would never trouble himself with such an errand; he would simply send his secretary. And I cannot imagine that you want to be trussed up in those fancy clothes again."

Wilson put his hand to his throat as he remembered the constricting collar and cravat.

"And besides," I said, pausing at the door of the back office, "we need a thorough and detailed inventory of those five miniatures – dimensions, materials, subjects and so on – so that we can compare them with the new

233

ones when they arrive, to see whether they are by the same hand. Your note-taking is coming on well, but a little more practice would not go amiss."

In truth, my real motive for leaving Wilson behind was my suspicion that the art tutor might be more forthcoming and honest in the company of a man like himself – a working lad made good, trying to better himself – than when grovelling to a titled gentleman.

The green door to the art tutor's staircase in Bateman's Buildings was ajar, perhaps left so by a less scrupulous tenant or visitor. I walked up three floors and was rather more surprised to find the attic room door likewise ajar. I knocked on it and, receiving no answer, went in. There was a stale odour in the room, due in no small part to the heavy curtains drawn across the windows and blocking all ventilation. I walked over to the large window – the one Bonneville used to light his work – and pushed the curtain aside a little, but the window was fixed with no opening. I turned to try another, and spied a shape lying on the bed against the wall. Too solid to be rumpled bedding, I knew immediately that it was a body. I bent over it, peering at the face turned to the wall. It was Bonneville, and he was dead.

Just then I heard someone running lightly up the stairs. The door was pushed open and in came the dirty little maid who had shown us in on our previous visits, with a paper packet in her hands. She thrust it at me.

"Powders, sir, for the master. He sent me for them. He's had terrible pains in his middle, sir, cramping that made him cry out."

I took the packet from her and she looked over at the bed and then dropped heavily into a chair.

"He's gone, isn't he, sir?" I nodded. "Poor man – he suffered something awful."

"Suffered in what way?" I asked.

"He said it was like someone twisting up his insides." She laid a hand on her own stomach. "Terrible sickness too, sir, and, well, everything like water, he said. When he asked me to rinse his underclothes, they were soiled like a baby's, sir." She looked up at me with wide eyes. "Is it something catching, do you think, sir? Will I catch it from touching him?" She held her hands out in front of her and then wiped them on her grubby skirt.

"What's your name, girl?" I asked.

"Jenny," she said. "Jenny Denton."

"From what you say, Jenny, I think it more like to be something Mr Bonneville ate or drank. Did you cook for him?"

Jenny shook her head. "Oh no, sir. Mr Bonneville was particular about his food – said it was because he was French, and I can only cook plain English. He ate out most days, and sometimes the young French lady would bring him a dish."

"Young French lady?" I asked. "Do you know her name?"

The maid shook her head again. "Lovely looking, though, she was – red hair, all curling."

"Did this French lady bring Mr Bonneville a dish to-day?" I asked.

"Not today, no, nor yesterday neither – I'd say three days ago. I washed up the dish for her to collect when she next comes." Jenny jumped up and went to the cupboard. "Here it is: always made me laugh, this one."

She handed me a pink and white dish, the two carry-ing handles in the shape of large spotted jungle cats, and the handle of the lid in the form of a leaping fish.

"Constable Plank, I am afraid that my father is not at home, nor in the bank, but calling on friends," said Sylvie Renard.

"That is no matter, Miss Renard," I said. "My business today is to return something to you." I handed her the pink and white dish, wrapped in a cloth I had retrieved from Bonneville's room. I watched her carefully as she unwrapped it, but her face showed only puzzlement.

"Do you know where I found that?" I asked.

"I took it to Monsieur Bonneville, a friend of my fa-ther's, on Saturday," she said easily. "He lives alone and craves the meals of his childhood; whenever I make a par-ticular daube of which he is fond – a rich stew – I always take care to send some to him." She turned to put the dish on the sideboard. "It is very kind of you to return it for him but this is not the job of a constable, no? Delivery boy?" She indicated a pair of chairs and we both sat.

"You are right, Miss Renard – the return of the dish is not the purpose of my visit. I am very sorry to have to tell you that Mr Bonneville has died." She put a hand to her mouth and straightened her back, but made no comment. "It seems that he had an internal complaint, and he died earlier today. His maid reported the matter to Great Marlborough Street, I was sent find out more, and when I saw the dish in his room I recognised the design. The maid's description of it being delivered by a young French lady with curling red hair could mean only you."

Miss Renard crossed herself and murmured, "May God have mercy on his soul."

"Food poisoning," said Martha, her hands on her hips as she surveyed her own spotless kitchen. "Well, what can you expect, with a bachelor living in those mucky conditions, eating goodness only knows what from goodness only knows where."

I winked at Wilson. "I think that is a warning meant for you," I said.

"Don't be foolish, Samuel Plank," said my wife. "William eats either here or at home. That poor Mr Bonneville had no wife or mother to care for him."

"But he had Sylvie," said Wilson miserably. Martha and I exchanged a glance over his head. "She never told me that she was cooking meals for him."

That caught my attention. "Did Miss Renard know that we knew Bonneville? Did you tell her?"

Wilson shook his head. "No. But she should have told me about her friendship with another man, don't you think?"

Martha squeezed his shoulder. "He was a friend of her father's, William," she said soothingly. "No doubt she saw him as an uncle and nothing more. But what did you think, Sam, when you saw that funny dish sitting there? Did you wonder whether that was the food…" She left the question unfinished.

"I've eaten Miss Renard's food, my love, and it is delicious. Not as good as yours, of course, but not far short. And prepared with care."

"But if it were left out uncovered, and something got into it?" asked Martha. I knew what she was really asking: was Miss Renard a poisoner?

"No: I considered that, but Jenny – the maid – said that Bonneville had eaten Miss Renard's food three days earlier. Food poisoning comes on almost straight away, and he was taken ill only yesterday."

We fell silent for a few moments. "With Bonneville gone," said Wilson suddenly, "who will fulfil the orders?"

CHAPTER TWENTY-NINE

Safely beyond all reach

WEDNESDAY 21ST MARCH 1827

When Wilson came into the back office the next morning and saw our visitor, he blinked several times.

"Constable Wilson, this is Mr Frederick Smith, junior customs officer at the Pennington Street bonded warehouse," I said. "And twin brother to Mr William Smith, whom we met some nights ago in St James."

Wilson sat opposite the young clerk and stared. "Forgive me," he said, "but I find identical twins rather unsettling."

"One of the skills a constable must learn, Mr Smith," I explained, "is to memorise faces so that they can reliably be recognised again. This skill is quite confounded when two faces are identical."

"No matter," said Smith. "Even our own mother, God rest her soul, was often unable to tell us apart. All I can offer is this." He lifted his head and indicated a scar on the point of his chin. "Perhaps Will was as keen as I that people should not confuse us, or maybe it was just his usual bad temper, but either way, thanks to his fist I have this scar and he does not."

"You do not share his bad temper?" I asked.

"I do not, sir, no," said the clerk, shaking his head. "It has amused the Almighty to make my brother and me as unalike in temperament as we are alike in appearance. From when we were in swaddling bands Will and I were as different as you can imagine – he the adventurer and I much more cautious."

"A distinction evident in your choice of work," I observed.

"Our father is a mercer," said Smith, "and determined that my brother and I should do better for ourselves. There was too much lifting and carrying in the shop, father always said, and then working on the ledgers late into the night. He taught us both the rudiments of bookkeeping, and – through the kind offices of the husband of a regular customer, who knew of our difficulties after the death of our mother – we both obtained positions in the customs service. For me, it could not have

been a happier match, but Will chafed against the re-
strictions, and, well, you know the rest."

"We do indeed, Mr Smith," I said. "What we do not
know is why you have come to see us."

The clerk leaned forward in his chair, clasping his
hands together until the knuckles showed white. "Constable Plank, my brother has fled London. He came home
the morning after you spoke to him, the maid said, took
a few items of clothing and left."

I remembered how reluctant William Smith had been
to tell us the name of the man controlling him. Pascal
Renard had not struck me as ruthless or violent, but revolutionary fervour can inflame the steadiest of men.

"Are you sure that your brother has gone away?" I
asked. "I do not wish to alarm you, but he was involved
with some unpleasant people who have much at stake."

"Constable Plank, I am a cautious man but not an innocent one: you cannot work long in Pennington Street
without learning what men will do to protect themselves." He dropped his head. "Remember, I saw what
happened to Mr Sharpe." He sighed. "I have of course
considered the possibility that Will has been abducted, or
worse. But we are, underneath it all, twin brothers, and
I believe I should know if he were dead. And anyway, he
left me a note."

"Do you have this note?" I asked.

Smith shook his head. "I burned it – but it would have been of no use to you in any case. It was written in a code that we have used since we were boys, and said simply that he was going to Southampton to find passage overseas. It was a long-cherished plan of his, to see the world. It will suit him, the vagabond life." The clerk sat upright. "And it is because he is now safely beyond all reach that I can come to you today. While Will was at Custom House and I at Pennington Street, we sometimes discussed our work. Being concerned with the assessment and collecting of duties, I was interested to hear about what happened to the submissions we made to the Long Room, and Will was likewise curious about how cargoes were checked and recorded." He looked at me and I nodded in encouragement. "One of the things I told him of was Mr Sharpe's routines – when he checked the vaults, how the vaults were protected and so on. Since that morning," he closed his eyes and swallowed hard, "since the attack, I have feared that Will took the information I gave him and passed it on to those who laid in wait for Mr Sharpe. May God forgive us both."

"Dear God, Martha, I cannot tell you the relief I feel," I said as we sat at our table that evening. Wilson had just left clutching a honey cake that Martha had made to celebrate his sister Janey's thirteenth birthday; my wife knew that sweet treats were a rarity in the little attic in

Brill Row where Wilson lived with his widowed mother and several siblings, but made sure to preserve their dignity by saying that the cake was our present to Janey.

Martha laid her hand over mine. "I know," she said gently.

"All these weeks I have feared that it was my message to Ben that had led his attackers to him, and now to discover that their plans were already laid, that it was simply a coincidence..." I shook my head. "I have been too ashamed to visit him, you know."

Of course she knew. "Then that is what you shall do tomorrow," she said, "and you can tell him what you have learned. Mr Sharpe is a professional man too, and I am sure it has been perplexing him, wondering how his movements were known and how his attackers made their escape so easily. No doubt they used the same scheme to waylay poor Mr King, with even unhappier consequences. You can put Mr Sharpe's mind at rest, as well as your own." She lifted my hand and kissed it, and I felt more worthy of that kiss than I had for some time.

CHAPTER THIRTY

Determination

THURSDAY 22ND MARCH 1827

B en Sharpe's home was just around the corner from the meagre lodgings rented by the late Mr King, but the contrast between the two dwellings could not have been greater. Ben and his wife occupied a set of rooms on the ground floor of a building of three storeys. Instead of a dingy yard with a truculent landlady, their rooms looked out onto a neat space with scrubbed flagstones, its edges lined with little troughs raised on bricks and planted with all manner of herbs which scented the air. Tucked into a corner of the yard, so positioned as to catch as much sun and as little wind as possible, was an old wicker chair lined with a blanket and with a low crate placed in front of it to serve as a footstool. As I looked at this cosy arrangement, the back door opened and out came my friend, leaning heavily on two sticks and taking small, shuffling steps, but undeniably walking.

"Ben!" I called out in gladness.

He looked up, and smiled in welcome. "Sam," he said. "Come and join me – you cannot imagine how tired I am of my own company. Peggy has gone out on her errands and I fancied some tea, but with these dratted things I find I cannot do much except hobble from chair to chair, and I cannot carry anything. And I much prefer to sit out here; years in those vaults have given me a great fondness for the open air, even in March." He reached the wicker seat and dropped heavily into it, letting his sticks fall to the floor with a clatter. I picked them up for him, leaning them against the wall within reach, and then went indoors to heat the water and make us a drink. Peggy and Martha were cut from the same cloth when it came to household organisation, and I was able to find my way around the tidy little kitchen with no difficulty.

"I confess that I am astonished to see you walking at all," I said, once we were both settled with a cup of tea and a slice of seed loaf (hidden in a cupboard, but Ben directed me to it). "The last we heard from Mrs Sharpe, you were not expected to make such a recovery."

"What do surgeons know?" said Ben dismissively. "They know to saw bones and apply leeches, and if they cannot do either of those, they give up."

"I am sure that is not true," I said.

Ben shrugged. "Near enough. I am a great believer in the mind, Sam," and he tapped his head for emphasis. "Determination, that is what is needed. I have made up my mind to walk again, and my body obeys. Slowly, to be sure, but it obeys. I will always limp, I know that – the kicks to my hips caused a lot of damage – but limping is still walking."

"And your work?" I asked.

"I will not be able to return to all the duties I had before – it would take me all day to go up and down those steps to the vaults. But I am promised work in the offices, probably instructing clerks."

"That will suit you, I think," I said. "You have the patience for it. Young Frederick Smith is certainly fond of you."

Ben looked at me. "Smith? Why do you mention him?"

I put my cup down. "He came to see me yesterday. He had some information that may help us to find your attackers. Did you know he has an identical twin brother?"

Ben smiled. "I did – William, isn't it? He called in once or twice to visit his brother – made me think I was seeing double after sniffing a bit too much brandy."

"And that this brother used to work at Custom House?" I asked.

"Used to? I did not know that he had left," said Ben.

"Some months ago, in less than happy circumstances,"
I said, "and I am afraid has fallen in with some rum coves.
It seems that Smith – your Smith – told his brother something of your routines, and this information was passed
to those who wished to warn you off." Ben stayed silent.
"In my view," I continued, "it would serve little to dismiss
Smith, although of course that is for you to decide. For
my part, as a constable, he has been extremely – if belat-
edly – helpful, making enquiries of all manner of people
at the warehouse. He has found that six men obtained
tasting permits for the evening before you were attacked,
and arrived as arranged – they were the only visitors that
night. Only five men left; armed with knowledge about
the shifts, they made sure that they arrived during one
watch shift and left during the next, so that a different
watchman was on duty when they left and they convinced
him that the earlier one had miscounted. The man who
stayed behind, we think, moved some barrels so that he
could reach the trap-door in the corner and unlock it –
Smith had mentioned to his brother that there was a trap-
door in case of emergency. At some point during the
night his two companions joined him, and they laid in
wait for you, knowing that you would come down alone
soon after eight in the morning."

"A clever scheme indeed," said Ben.

"And one for which young Smith now feels entirely responsible," I said. "But if a man cannot trust his own brother…"

Ben held up his hand to stop me. "You need not fear that I will punish Smith," he said. "He has come good now, when much the easiest course of action would have been to say nothing." He paused for a moment. "Is that how they gained entry to kill King, and escaped afterwards?"

"We think so, yes," I replied. I took a deep breath. "Ben," I said, "I have my own reason for being grateful to Smith. For some time, I have feared that it was my message to you that alerted the attackers to your suspicions, and that told them when and where you would be that morning. The guilt has been a weight on me. It is perhaps unmanly of me to admit it, but I am glad that the fault is someone else's and not mine."

Ben smiled gently. "You have always felt too deeply, Sam – it makes you a good champion for the unfortunate but, as you say, it can weigh heavily on you. Had I known that it was worrying you so, I could have put your mind to rest about that wretched note: it arrived here later that same morning. The message lad you chose was not wicked, merely slow and easily distracted. And as the time for the meeting you proposed had already passed, Peggy did not think to send the note on to me at Pennington Street."

I shook my head and smiled. "I shall make sure to select only swift, determined lads in future."

Ben leaned forward. "Sam," he said seriously, "the facts are these: I was attacked but have survived, and my clerk was unfortunately involved but has confessed. The best use of your skills now is to find who did it – and why. What were they concerned we would uncover if we looked into the death of Mr King? Why should a couple of Frenchmen care about the death of an English customs officer?"

I blinked. "Frenchmen, you say? But the man I heard giving the orders was English, I'm sure of it."

Ben nodded. "Oh yes, he was – but his two brutes were French, yammering away to each other."

"Do you speak French?" I asked.

"Only enough to communicate with French captains – mostly words to do with cargoes. And of course I was not in the best shape at the time, so I could not make much sense of what was said to me in English, let alone French. I did hear a couple of words repeated a few times, though: revolution, and 'la maitresse'."

Conant walked his fingers along the spines of the books until he came to the one he wanted. "It's my grandfather's Cotgrave dictionary, rather elderly now, but it will suffice," he said, taking it off the shelf and across to the table.

"It must be a great relief for you to see your friend recovering, and in such good spirits."

"It is, sir," I said. "His children are grown, but he would have left a widow – and friends who would miss him. As it is, the customs service is to make some financial recompense for his injuries because he was on duty when he was attacked, and he can continue to work in the offices at Pennington Street."

The magistrate nodded. "Ah, yes, here we are: 'maitresse'. As I thought. Mistress, of school or of house."

"Who could they have meant?" I asked.

"Well, in French, as in many European languages, nouns are assigned a gender," said Conant. "So 'le livre' is masculine," he gestured to the book he was reading, "while 'la chaise'", pointing to the chair, "is feminine. It seems to have little rhyme or reason to it, beyond the obvious – cow being feminine and bull being masculine and so on."

I nodded. "I remember puzzling over this in Mrs Plank's primer."

"And you said that the other word that Mr Sharpe overheard was 'revolution'," he continued. "And 'la révolution' is feminine, so perhaps that is 'la maitresse' to which they were referring: revolution as the mistress who directs their actions."

CHAPTER THIRTY-ONE

Lagrange comes to town

MONDAY 26TH MARCH 1827

Four days later we had the answer to Wilson's question about who would replace Bonneville, when we received a message for Lord Nameless, again delivered via his gambling club.

"My dear sir," said the note, "I am grieved to have to tell you of the sudden passing of Monsieur Bonneville. You may rest assured, however, that our recent agreement will be honoured, and a delivery will be effected next week by Monsieur Lagrange. I will write again with more details when they are known. I remain humbly yours, Pascal Renard."

"Lagrange?" said Wilson. "The Frenchman you met in Sittingbourne? But I thought he refused to come to London."

"With Bonneville gone, Renard is having to think quickly if he is to meet the demand for these paintings," I said. "I daresay he has impressed upon Lagrange the urgency of the situation – reminded him that his own cut of the profits relies on timely delivery – and our country boy's qualms about visiting the city have been overridden."

And indeed, six days later, as promised by Renard, another message was delivered to Lord Nameless, this time confirming that three new miniatures had been acquired by Lagrange, who would be staying at the Three Nuns on Aldgate High Street for the night of Tuesday the 3rd of April, should Lord Nameless care to arrange for collection of the paintings.

CHAPTER THIRTY-TWO

The Three Nuns

TUESDAY 3RD APRIL 1827

On the afternoon of the Tuesday I once more assumed my disguise as John Snaith, secretary to his Lordship, and once more Wilson turned down his mouth at being left out of the adventure.

The Three Nuns is a fair journey from Great Marlborough Street, and I sent a message home to Martha to warn her that I would be late returning and would miss my dinner. It was a pleasant day, with the promise of spring in the air, and I resolved to walk part of the way and then complete my journey by coach, in case Lagrange should see me arrive – the secretary of a man such as Lord Nameless would not conduct his business on foot. A magistrate's constable, now, that was another matter. Although I was not in uniform I still had my eyes and ears on duty, and there is nothing more instructive to a constable than regular immersion in the society around him. On my walk I noted which shops were flourishing and which struggling, which taverns were full and which empty, and whose ladybirds were popular and whose out of favour. Both success and struggle will alter a man's behaviour, and it is as well for any student of motive to keep abreast of these matters.

With so much to occupy and divert me, I soon found myself at Holborn and engaged a jarvey on the stand in Leather Lane. As we rattled through the streets, I quickly re-read the notes I had made after my meeting with Lagrange in Sittingbourne before slipping my notebook deep into an inside pocket of my coat.

At the Three Nuns I spoke to the landlord and he directed me to a private parlour off the main rooms. I remembered the snug at the Rose Inn; the agent was obviously careful where he conducted his business. Sitting in the parlour, a ledger open on his knees but unseen, as he was staring at the fire, was Antoine Lagrange.

"Mr Lagrange," I said.

He quickly closed the ledger and rose to his feet, his hand outstretched to shake mine. He was as I remembered – the wild hair, the broken nose – and the same was obviously true in reverse, as he greeted me immediately.

"Monsieur Sneth," he said. "Come: join me in a drink." He indicated the other chair before the fire and then put his head round the door and called for the potboy. Once our tankards were filled, Lagrange raised his towards me. "Your good health, sir – santé, as we say."

"Santé," I echoed. "I was sorry to hear about Mr Bonneville," I said after a moment. "He was a friend of yours?"

Lagrange shrugged. "Not a friend, exactly, no, monsieur. But we knew each other professionally – he had what we call a good eye, an ability to discern fine pieces, and it is a loss. And the manner of his death," the agent shuddered, "it was not pleasant, no?"

"No?" I asked, remembering just in time that Snaith would know only what Renard had said in his message.

Lagrange pointed at his stomach. "All twisted – terrible pain."

I shook my head and then raised my tankard. "To Mr Bonneville, then," I said, "and to his good eye."

Lagrange nodded, saluted the fire with his own tankard, and then drank deeply. After a minute or two he seemed to recall the purpose of our meeting and reached down beside his chair, lifting a leather bag onto his lap.

"I think," he said, opening the flap of the bag and rummaging around inside it, "your young master will be particularly pleased with what I have found for him this time." He pulled from the bag a small package wrapped in cloth and string and handed it to me. "Here." He passed me a small knife from the plate sitting on the table beside him. It was a sharp little thing and made short work of the string. Inside the parcel were three miniatures, two ovals of young women alone, and one rectangular piece showing a group of three bathing under a waterfall. It would not do for me to show too much interest, beyond checking the quality of the pieces, but as I made to wrap them again, Lagrange reached across and stayed my hand.

"This one is the finest, no?" he said, pointing at one of the individual portraits. "I like her... bravery." In the painting, the young woman was bare to the waist but, instead of pretending that she was unseen, she looked boldly, even defiantly, towards the artist. "Unusual, no?" I nodded. "And in recognition of this," said Lagrange smoothly, "the price will be a little higher than before." I opened my mouth but the agent held up a hand. "Show her to your master. If he does not wish to pay the higher price, then he can simply return her to us. There is no obligation to buy. But he will, monsieur – he will."

Lagrange invited me to stay for dinner but I had no wish to prolong our meeting; a man in disguise often gives himself away with over-confidence, and the longer we talked and the more I drank, the more risks I took that I might give away my true identity. So I wrapped up the miniatures and took my leave of the Frenchman.

In the coach on the way home, I realised that my stomach was rumbling and, with my dinner no doubt already fed to Wilson, I decided to kill two birds with one stone and stop at the Blue Boar in Holborn for refreshment and to call on Alice. The coaching inn was as bustling as ever, and when I gave my name to the potboy and asked him to summon his master, I had to wait a good ten minutes before George Atkins arrived.

"Constable Plank," he said with a welcoming smile, wiping his hands on his apron and then reaching out to shake mine. Unlike many of his breed, this innkeeper was lean of build, his thinness emphasised by his height. He had once confided to me, almost shamefacedly, that he could not abide the taste of ale, and no doubt that kept his weight down, and his profits up. "All is well, I trust, with you and your lady wife?"

"Mrs Plank is in fine health, thank you," I replied. "And Mrs Atkins, and your little ones?"

"All thriving, saints be praised," said the innkeeper. "No doubt you wish to see Alice?"

"If she is not abed," I said.

Atkins gave a snort of laughter. "Abed? With little Martha so keen to try her new legs? Poor Alice has resorted to keeping her on a string, like a dog, otherwise the little imp disappears the moment her mother turns her back. Alice will be grateful for the distraction, I am sure. Now, you settle yourself in the back parlour – the front one is crammed with a coach-load eating dinner – and I will send Alice to you, and a tray of food. And now you must excuse me: the timetable is an unforgiving master, and that coach must be on its way in seven minutes."

The innkeeper dashed off towards the kitchen and I went into the back parlour and looked out of the window onto the yard which was, as ever, full of fevered yet controlled activity. A few minutes later I heard Alice coming down the corridor, talking to her little girl. The door opened and in they came. Alice was obviously thriving on life as a nurserymaid in the Blue Boar, although I have found that any kind of work can be rewarding as long as it is valued and those doing it are treated with kindness. And for kindness, it would be hard to match that offered by the innkeeper and his wife. The haunted look had gone from Alice's eyes, there was a ready smile on her lips, and it was with confidence and pride that she held her infant daughter on her hip. For her part, little Martha – now almost a year old – was a wriggling, curious bundle. She put out her arms to me, seeing me as a means of escaping from her mother's grasp, and Alice passed her over before quickly shutting the parlour door.

"Put her down before she kicks you," she said laughingly. "She's found her legs and wants nothing but to explore."

"She's blooming, Alice, as are you," I said as we both watched Martha totter over to the chair near the window and peer underneath it.

"Thank you, Mr Plank," Alice replied. She often forgot that I was a constable – to her, I was simply the husband of one of her dearest friends – and I preferred not to remind her. "And Mrs Plank is well? We met a few weeks ago, to take little Martha to toddle around in Lincoln's Inn Fields."

"Big Martha is fine," I said, smiling. "Her work with the girls at school keeps her busy these days, but I think it does her good."

"And them, Mr Plank – they are lucky to have her." Alice glanced down at her daughter, who was now inspecting the laces of my boot. "And William – he is well too?"

"Ah, well, things are not as happy with Wilson as we might hope," I said, indicating that we should sit.

Alice perched on the edge of one of the chairs, always with an eye on Martha. The little girl went towards the door, reaching for the knob, and Alice said "No" in a low voice and held up her right hand. Tied around the wrist was a piece of string. "I have found that simply reminding her that I could attach her to me sometimes has the desired effect," said Alice. And indeed, little Martha turned away from the door and instead walked wide-legged to the table. "Is William unwell?"

"Not physically, no," I said, and explained a little of what had happened with Miss Renard. "And so he is disappointed, and heart-sore, and embarrassed," I finished.

"Poor Will," said Alice, leaning down to catch Martha as she passed. She sat her daughter on her knees and straightened the little girl's clothes. "Perhaps Martha and I should go and visit him, see if we can't make him laugh. Would you like to see Uncle Will?" She smiled at the little girl and then looked across at me. "You would think he'd have had enough of little ones, with his own brother and sisters, but he always has time for Martha."

"Practice, I daresay," I said. "And I think a visit from this young lady might be just the tonic for him."

There was a knock, and the potboy came in with a laden tray. Little Martha's eyes grew round as she watched him unload everything onto the table, and Alice kept tight hold of her chubby hands to stop her reaching out. The last plate had on it a generous slice of cake, which the child obviously recognised, if her gurgle of delight was anything to go by.

"And now we will leave you in peace, Mr Plank," said Alice, getting to her feet and hoisting little Martha onto her hip. "This one will start to grizzle soon, and you will not thank me if you end up with grubby little hand-marks on your fine coat and trousers. Please give my dearest regards to Mrs Plank, and tell Will that we will see him soon."

I had just finished the rather good chop and potatoes and was contemplating the cake when I heard a commotion in the corridor, with people shouting and doors banging. Outside the window, a group of coachmen had gathered in the yard and were gesticulating excitedly towards the street. I stuck my head out of the door and stopped the potboy as he galloped past.

"What on earth is going on, lad? Is there a fire in the kitchen?"

"No, sir," he said breathlessly. "But someone has just arrived with the news: they've caught Anthony Houseman. He was lodging for the night at the Three Nuns in Aldgate, bold as you like."

"The Three Nuns?" I repeated. "Are you sure? I was there earlier this evening myself."

The potboy looked desperately back down the corridor – he was obviously on hot coals to hear the latest. "Definitely, sir – he was found in the parlour just below the picture of the three nuns at prayer." He dropped his voice conspiratorially. "They were lucky to catch him, sir. In disguise he was. Hair all long, they say, and pretending to be a Frenchie!"

"Thank you, lad – you can go," I said, but I found myself talking to his back as he raced off.

"A highwayman?" said Martha as we sat over a pot of tea. "I told you, you see – I told you it was dangerous.

And there you were, in the same room, and him with a knife!" She shook her head.

"Not like the highwaymen of old, my dear – this was no Jack Sheppard," I said soothingly. "But he is still famous enough for his name to be known in coaching inns, even by a potboy at the Blue Boar who was not yet born when Houseman gave up the road. He simply disappeared. According to Mr Atkins, the story at the time was that Houseman sensed that his luck was running out, what with armed guards on the coaches and gates on the turnpikes, and he did not fancy the gibbet. And the knife he had tonight, my dear, was for his cheese, not his former trade. It was Houseman's bad luck that he chose to stay last night at the same coaching inn as someone he had robbed on the road years ago and who had a good memory for faces."

"Was that why he refused to come into London, do you think?" Martha asked.

"Almost certainly," I agreed. "Atkins said that Houseman was notorious on the roads to Exeter and Penzance, so I daresay he reasoned that he was less likely to be recognised if he stayed in Kent. And the coaches for those destinations depart from, I believe, the Bull and Mouth in St Martin's Lane, not far from here, so when Renard ordered him to come to London he chose to stay in an inn to the east instead – but then his luck ran out."

"So your Monsieur Lagrange is not French at all," said Martha, staring into the bottom of her cup.

"He's no more French than I am," I said, "for all his accent and his pretence. He's from Hounslow."

CHAPTER THIRTY-THREE

Home to roost

WEDNESDAY 4TH APRIL 1827 – MORNING

"Ah yes, Hounslow Heath was notorious for highway robbery, was it not, Sam?" said Conant, as I made my report to him the next morning. I had brought Wilson with me; as a reward for his good work on our excursion to Herne Bay, the magistrate had suggested that Wilson should be present for all deliberations concerning our interest in French miniatures. Wilson was quite puffed up with the honour.

"It was, sir," I confirmed. "For many years, Constable Wilson, it was considered the most dangerous place in England. The roads to Exeter and Bath cross the heath, whose open expanses gave the highwayman plenty of room for escape. And travelling on those roads were wealthy visitors to the resorts in the West Country, and courtiers returning to Windsor – all of whom provided rich pickings for those who preyed on them."

"And Mr Houseman, being from the area, would have known all about it," said Wilson shyly.

"Indeed, constable, indeed," agreed Conant. "I venture that he might even have served an apprenticeship of sorts under an experienced man." He shook his head and smiled. "Lagrange is French for grand house, of course – Houseman. He had a sense of mischief. Do you suppose, Constable Wilson, that Renard knew that his agent was English, not French?"

Wilson flushed slightly as we both turned to look at him, the magistrate and I. He was used to discussing such possibilities with me, but to be asked his view by Mr Conant was something new for him. I willed him to answer.

"I suspect that he did, sir." He stopped.

"And why is that?" asked Conant.

"Because – because Lagrange might have sounded French to us, but would it have fooled a Frenchman? And what if Renard spoke to him in French?"

Conant nodded. "He could have learned the language, but we English always retain an accent, I am told, which gives us away. Which leads us to another consideration: if Renard knew that Lagrange – Houseman – was English, did he also know that he was a wanted man?"

The Newgate turnkey's face twisted into a smile when I stated my business.

"It's like the old days, isn't it, sir, you coming here to visit a gentleman of the road," he said, hauling open the door and beckoning me in. He pushed it shut and slid home the substantial bolt before being true to his name and turning the key in the lock. He tested the door by pulling on it and then led me through the courtyard towards the slightly less dismal part of the prison known as the State Apartments. "Aye," said the turnkey, anticipating my question, "there are plenty nostalgic for the glamour of the highwayman, and some of them are foolish enough to pay his garnish. Although Mr Wontner has forbidden easement – Mr Houseman has too many friends who would be willing to help him escape."

"I thought to call on Mr Wontner first," I said, gesturing towards his office.

"The keeper is on his rounds already, sir, and says that he will join you with the prisoner."

We climbed a staircase and walked along a corridor. Halfway along the turnkey knocked on a door and a severe-faced woman answered. She looked me up and down and showed no pleasure at what she saw.

"Mrs Appleton, this is Constable Samuel Plank of Great Marlborough Street, come to visit Houseman," said the turnkey.

She closed the door in our faces.

"You must not mind her," said the turnkey quietly. "She has spent her entire life here in Newgate. Her mother provided marital comforts," he paused to check that I had apprehended his meaning, "to the wealthier prisoners, and this one was the result. She tried life outside but it didn't take and back she came. Married a gaoler and carries on his duties now that he has gone. Good at heart, but it hardens you, this place."

The door opened again and out came the lady gaoler. "Now that you have finished telling my business to all and sundry, Mr Browne, shall we call on Mr Houseman?" She led us to the end of the corridor and pulled up the bunch of keys hanging from her waist. "Mr Browne forgets, Constable Plank, that we gaolers hear everything."

She opened the door and ushered me in; Browne touched his forehead and shambled off back to his post.

"Visitor, Mr Houseman," she said to the shape lying on the bed. "I shall have to lock you in, constable – orders of Mr Wontner. Bang on the door when you are ready to leave."

I have heard it many times, but the sound of a prison door closing behind me and then the key being turned in the lock never fails to make me shiver. The occupant of the room stirred under his blanket, and carefully lowered his feet to the ground; the long chain connecting his ankle irons to the staple in the middle of the floor clanked and scraped as it settled into its new position.

"Constable, eh," said Houseman, lifting his head to look at me. Gone was the French accent, and gone too were the flowing locks, no doubt in deference to the robust population of lice that made their home in places such as this. The prisoner scratched his stubbly head and then let his hand fall as he stared at me. "Well, well – Mr Snaith, I do believe."

I nodded. "We are neither of us who we purported to be at our previous meetings, Mr Houseman." I picked up one of the two rickety chairs standing guard at an equally rickety table and placed it before the bed. "May I?" Houseman waved a gracious hand and I sat down.

"Are you come with a pardon from the King for me, Constable...?" he asked with a wry smile.

"Samuel Plank," I said, "Great Marlborough Street. And we both know how things will end for you, I am afraid, Mr Houseman. You are too late for the notoriety of Tyburn Tree by some forty years, but other equally final arrangements are now made for highway robbers." We both glanced at the single high window in the wall; somewhere beyond it was the yard where the scaffold would be raised when needed.

"I thought I had left that life behind me," said the prisoner. "Twenty years or more – and then to run into that man at the Three Nuns. Do you know, when I robbed him he was a grown man of about eighteen, and yet he hid behind his mother – his mother! – and offered me her jewels to leave him alone. He snivelled and wept like a woman." Houseman shook his head.

"Then it is no wonder that he is calling for justice, Mr Houseman – you witnessed his weakness, and his shame cries for revenge," I said.

Houseman looked at me for a long moment. "You are a student of men, Constable Plank," he said.

"It is true that I like to understand why people do what they do, yes," I replied. "And it is in pursuit of this that I come to see you today. We know that the French artist Louis Rambert was murdered."

"Murdered?" said Houseman in genuine surprise. "I thought he disturbed some robbers and was beaten, and died of his injuries."

I shook my head. "No: it was made to look that way, but he was stabbed – here." I pointed just below my heart.

"Poor fellow," said the prisoner sadly. "He had a deal of sadness in his life, but his portraits – they were the finest I have seen."

"How long did he work for you?" I asked.

Houseman looked at me and sighed deeply; I think it was then that he decided to unburden himself. Even the wickedest of men find it difficult to die with a heavy conscience, and I could tell that the one before me was not the wickedest of men. "About ten years," he said.

"And how did you meet Mr Rambert?"

"I met his work first," replied Houseman. "In one of my robberies I relieved a gentleman of four miniature portraits in fine gold frames. Three of the paintings were poor things, and I discarded them in order to sell the frames, but the fourth was different. It showed a young woman with skin so glowing, eyes so bright – she almost leapt from the frame. The fellow begged to keep it, said it was his sweetheart who had died, painted by her London art tutor Louis Rambert. And soft-hearted fool that I am, I agreed. I could have sold it many times over, that one." He smiled sadly at me, and I knew that I had been right about his lack of wickedness. "A few years after that I changed my line of business – too many close encounters with a pepperbox for my liking. I moved to Kent to put some distance between me and Hounslow Heath, and spent my nights in the coaching inns, befriending weary travellers, sharing a tankard or two with them, and then relieving them of their burdensome valuables once they were asleep." He shrugged apologetically. "If it's all a man knows." I nodded. "And then one night I found myself with my arm behind my back and a knife under my ribs: he'd woken and found me going through his things."

"Who?" I asked.

"François Dejeune," said Houseman, his French accent returning. "Met a knife himself a couple of years later, but not before he had recruited me. In exchange for my freedom, I worked for him, although, to be honest, the work suited me and I liked it. Well, you met Antoine La-grange – did he not seem a man in his element?" I nodded. "The demand for French miniatures was inexhaustible," continued Houseman, "particularly when we introduced our more specialist subjects for gentlemen. We needed more artists and I remembered Rambert. We had some-one call on him and he was in a bad way – low on funds and in poor health. We offered him work and he took it – what choice did he have? His portraits were as good as I remembered; to be honest, our customers were paying a fair price for them, such was their quality, even though they thought they were buying old family pieces from France. But Rambert refused to paint the more risqué portraits – he said he did not want to look at young women in that way. And then we heard of the robbery."

"The murder, Mr Houseman," I reminded him. "Per-haps Mr Dejeune's successor was not willing to tolerate Rambert's refusal to paint what he was told." Houseman shrugged. "And who is that successor, Mr Houseman?"

"For the past seven years or so, I have received my or-ders from Pierre Bonneville, and – as John Snaith will re-member – we communicate through the banker Renard."

There was the sound of the key turning in the lock and the door was opened to admit John Wontner.

"Thank you, Mrs Appleton," he said and our hostess withdrew once more and locked us in. The keeper waited until her footsteps had faded before saying with a shudder, "That woman's refined tones quite unnerve me." He picked up the other chair and brought it over to us, sitting at an angle to accommodate his wooden leg. "When she was a girl, some of our more educated prisoners amused themselves by teaching her to read and write and converse. Much as I approve of education for girls," he nodded at me, "I do wonder whether this contributed to her inability to settle into life outside Newgate – with that background and that education, she was neither fish nor fowl. Now, where are we?"

"Mr Houseman was just explaining to me how he came to be involved in selling people miniatures painted in England while pretending that they had come from France," I said.

"Always give the customer what he wants, Constable Plank," said the prisoner. "And our customers want to believe that they are acquiring rare and valued works from old French families – it gives them cachet." I raised a questioning eyebrow. "Hard to translate: uniqueness, perhaps, rarity."

"And the other more specialist pieces, as you put it?" I asked. "Surely an English young lady in a state of undress is just as desirable as her French cousin?"

Houseman looked at me and smiled. "Come now, constable – I do not need to tell a man of the world such as yourself that the unfamiliar is always more exciting. It adds a frisson – a thrill of daring." I thought of poor Wilson and how captivated he had been by Miss Renard, and this reminded me that there were more victims in this than Houseman might care to acknowledge. "Of course, although our customers believe the girls to be French, most of them were English, as you know, Constable Plank. That was a clever idea, to look for young ladies at that school."

"There are always those willing to exploit the worthy intentions and good deeds of others," I said, thinking of my dear wife and her horror at seeing Jane Caldwell in that painting. "It is not to your credit, sir." Houseman had the good grace to hang his head. "And so to convince any customers who might ask that their paintings had indeed been brought in from France," I continued, "you came up with the idea of taking the paintings to Kent, loading them onto ships heading up the Thames, and forging Customs House receipts."

"I cannot take all the credit for that idea either," said Houseman quickly. "I had made some friends in Kent who were adept at the movement of cargo, and one of them suggested the scheme. And in any grand enterprise like the customs service, there are always those whose assistance can be bought."

"Robert King," I said. Houseman nodded. "And do you think that his death was also a botched robbery?" I asked.

"No, sir – but please believe that there was nothing I could do about that. When King started to lose his nerve and said that he would confess, the order came from Renard that he had to be killed; two French assassins were brought in especially."

"Perhaps the same men killed Rambert," I said.

Houseman shrugged again. "Perhaps. I do know that they attacked that other customs officer in the vaults when he started saying that he thought King might not have killed himself... It frightened me, if I am honest, sir, to see how ruthless Renard had become. Robbing a gentleman of his watch on Hounslow Heath is one thing, but murdering customs officers is quite another. I started to think of how to make my escape, but then Bonneville died and I was summoned to London, and, well, you know the rest." He gestured at the manacles on his legs.

Wontner sighed; it always distressed him to see a man brought low by his crimes. Despite years – decades – of dealing with London's felons, he retained an unshakable belief that man is essentially a moral creature, and it is this belief that kept John Wontner from becoming a cold-hearted, vicious monster like so many prison keepers.

"You have been a great help, Mr Houseman," he said, "a fact which shall be relayed to the magistrates by Constable Plank and to the judge by me, when the time comes. I doubt that it will keep you from the scaffold, for which you must prepare yourself, but every effort will be made."

Houseman held out his hand, and Wontner leaned forward and shook it. The keeper stood and banged on the door.

"Thank you, Mr Houseman," I said. "You were excellent company in Sittingbourne, and I am sorry that it has come to this."

Mrs Appleton unlocked the door and opened it.

"Do you have time for a drink, Sam?" asked Wontner as we walked to the door.

I pulled out my watch and peered at it in the gloom. "A quick one, but then I must be off to find Mr Renard in his banking house – he and I have much to discuss."

"Mr Renard?" called out Houseman. "Mr Renard, constable? I fear you mistake me: when I say that Renard was giving the orders, I do not mean the banker – I mean his daughter."

"His daughter?" I said, turning in astonishment. "You mean Miss Sylvie Renard?"

The prisoner nodded. "The very same."

"But you see why we were misled," said Wontner. "Why on earth would you refer to a young lady by her surname?"

"Renard's explicit instructions," said Houseman. "In Utopia, apparently, men and women are equal and must be treated the same."

CHAPTER THIRTY-FOUR

The broken banker

WEDNESDAY 4TH APRIL 1827 – AFTERNOON

M r Conant stared out of the window of his dining room, as he was wont to do when thinking deeply. I tried to stay still and silent, but I knew that time was of the essence: word would have reached Sylvie Renard that Houseman had been apprehended, and she might suspect – correctly – that he would give her away.

The magistrate turned to look at me. "So Miss Renard is the 'maitresse' of whom those two men were talking." He shook his head. "I am not accustomed, Sam, as you know, to interfere in the way you work. I grant you a latitude that is unusual for a magistrates' constable. But I do wonder whether this time you are making an error of judgement in taking Constable Wilson with you. With his former attachment to Miss Renard, he might find this a difficult arrest."

"I am sure he will, sir," I said, "but that is not reason enough to exclude him. A constable must be able to put his own concerns aside in order to concentrate on the matter in hand. But I do not propose to take him simply in order to teach him a lesson: Constable Wilson knows Miss Renard better than I do, and she may feel more able to talk in his presence than mine."

Conant sighed. "Sam, I hope that you are right, but as the father of a young woman of similar age to Miss Renard, I fear that you are not. It will be a case not of her ability to talk, but rather of her willingness to do so." He walked over to the table and glanced down at the pile of papers there that, no matter how many hours he worked, never seemed to shrink. "Nonetheless, I am persauded: you will take Constable Wilson with you to the banking house, and here is a warrant for the arrest of Miss Sylvie Renard on suspicion of involvement in the murder of Robert King." He bent over the table and signed the top sheet on the pile, blew on it to dry the ink and handed it to me.

Wilson was silent as we walked along Wardour Street towards Pall Mall, barely acknowledging the merchants and tavern keepers who touched their caps and wished us a good afternoon. I left him to his thoughts until we turned into Craven Street.

"You know what we are to do, constable," I said calmly. "We have a warrant for the arrest of Miss Renard, so that she can be brought before the magistrate to answer this charge. A serious charge." Wilson nodded but still said nothing. I stopped and put a hand on his arm. "William, I am not insensible to the delicacy of the situation. You had a connection with the young lady, and this will no doubt be raised by the magistrates, which will be unpleasant. But there is no man alive – not even a magistrate, and certainly not a constable – who has not had a connection that he regrets. Thankfully you have the chance to make amends, and to make matters right before the court and – more importantly – with your own conscience." Wilson looked at me. "By entering the banking house with me, by watching me execute this warrant with you as my witness, and by remembering that you are, above all, a constable. It is not for us to judge Miss Renard, for which I think we are both grateful, but it is our duty to take her to those who will. Now, Constable Wilson, are you ready?"

"I am, sir, yes," said Wilson, and he straightened his back and squared his shoulders – a movement that caught the eye of a maid scrubbing the steps of a house nearby.

"Good afternoon, my handsome fellow," she called out.

A hint of a smile appeared on Wilson's face, and I thanked goodness for the resilience of a young man's heart.

Although it was an afternoon in the middle of the week, the door of the banking house of Burnham and Renard at number 37 was shut and locked. Wilson and I looked at each other, and he raised the knocker and banged loudly several times. The maid down the street looked in our direction. We waited a minute and then knocked again. This time we heard the bolt being drawn back, the door was opened a crack, and the pale, frightened face of a young man peered out at us.

"I am afraid that the banking house is closed today, sirs," he said. "A family matter, entirely unavoidable."

He made to shut the door, but Wilson put up a large hand and held it open.

"I am Constable Samuel Plank, of Great Marlborough Street," I said in a low tone, "and I require admittance. I have a warrant." I held up the folded piece of paper so that Mr Conant's signature was visible.

The young lad's eyes grew even larger and he swallowed hard before wordlessly opening the door. We stepped into the banking hall, which was empty and dim, as the shutters had not been opened.

"I wish to see Miss Sylvie Renard," I said. "I know the way," and I led Wilson to the back of the bank and up the narrow staircase. At the top the door to the dining room was slightly ajar, and I knocked before entering. Sitting in an armchair was Pascal Renard. He turned his head slowly to look at us.

"Constables," he said flatly. No longer the jovial, greedy man we had met two months earlier, the banker seemed broken. "Come in, gentlemen," he said. And then something occurred to him and he leapt to his feet. "Have you found her? Has something happened to my Sylvie? Please God, not the river!" He put a hand to his mouth and tears came to his eyes.

I glanced at Wilson, and I could tell from the set of his jaw that he was working hard to remember my advice: constable first.

I walked across to the banker and put a hand on his shaking shoulder. "It is about Miss Renard that we are come, yes, but we are surprised to find her gone." I handed him the paper; he took it with both hands but did not unfold it and simply looked at it uncomprehendingly. "It is a warrant for her arrest," I said gently.

"Arrest?" he repeated. "For a crime?"

"A customs officer, Mr Robert King, was killed on the 15th of February last, and it is suspected that Miss Renard was involved in organising his murder," I said.

The banker collapsed back into his chair, dropping the warrant onto the floor. "Murder? My Sylvie?" He looked at Wilson, seemingly noticing him for the first time. "And you – do you believe this? You know my Sylvie."

Wilson stepped forward and then, to my surprise, knelt by the side of the armchair and took one of the banker's hands in both of his. "It will break our hearts, sir, yours and mine, but yes, I think Sylvie is involved." Wilson took a breath and continued. "There is a chance that she is not involved, or that she is involved but against her will." The banker looked at me with hope in his eyes, and I nodded. "And if that is the case, sir," said Wilson, "Sylvie must come forward and explain. The warrant says simply that the magistrates wish to question her on this matter – not that she is committed for trial, and certainly not that her guilt is established." Wilson squeezed the banker's hand. "So please, sir, if you have any idea where she might be, you must tell us. It will go much better for her if we can find her and she comes forward."

"But William," said the banker, his voice breaking, "I do not know where she is. I came home late last night and she was gone. Her room is in disarray, some items taken but many left behind – she has gone on only a short trip, perhaps." He looked up at me, willing me to agree. "I was going to call on some of her friends, to ask them if they had seen Sylvie, but Mr Greenwood sent word first thing that he is indisposed, our junior clerk is not yet able to work unsupervised, and so you find me in chaos."

I picked up two dining chairs and placed them in front of the banker's armchair, sitting on one myself and indicating that Wilson should take the other.

"Mr Renard," I said, "it is not only the death of Mr King that concerns us. We are also aware that someone has been colluding with Mr Lagrange and the late Mr Bonneville to cheat your clients, by selling them paintings that..." But before I could finish, the banker had reared up out of his seat.

"Cheating my clients, you say?" he bellowed. "Cheating my clients?" Wilson stood, putting out a calming hand, but the banker knocked it away. "I have done no such thing, sir." He looked from me to Wilson and back again. "Who is it that accuses me of cheating?"

"Mr Renard," I said, "if you will please sit down, I will explain."

The banker sniffed with indignation, but sat as I requested.

"When I met Antoine Lagrange in Sittingbourne, and he agreed to seek out suitable miniature paintings in France for me, he gave your name as his banker," I said.

"But when you visited me and asked about Antoine, I explained that he was a friend, but not a client," said Renard.

"Indeed – but Lagrange suggested otherwise," I said. "And when I met the art tutor Pierre Bonneville and he offered to commission certain works for me, he also said that messages would be passed through you."

The banker looked confused. "But Pierre, again, a friend only – not a client. A much-missed friend. And he never passed any messages through me."

"So are you saying, sir," I said slowly, "that you know nothing of this dishonest trade in French miniatures?"

The banker shook his head vehemently. "I knew that Lagrange was engaged in the importation of French works of art, yes, but for honest sale. As for Bonneville, I knew only that he was an art tutor and a portrait painter – Sylvie mentioned that he visited your wife's school, Constable Plank, to teach them the rudiments of painting pretty pictures." I felt a shiver of revulsion as he said this, but tried hard not to show it. "I tried to help both men by passing on to them the names of any of my clients who had expressed an interest in the purchase of art. If their trade was dishonest, then, hélas, I have been as misled as you, and feel all the more foolish for it." He shook his head.

"When we first met you, Mr Renard," I said, "we asked whether you knew an artist called Louis Rambert, and you said that you did not."

The banker nodded. "I remember."

"But you did know him," I said.

"I did, yes." The banker sighed. "He was a fine artist, one of the finest, and a good man. But his son was not:

his son was a thief and a cheat, who stole money from many people in Rennes – their home in France. Monsieur Rambert brought his daughter-in-law and his grand-daughter to England to escape the shame, but they both died soon afterwards, leaving him alone. He never recovered." He shook his head sadly. "The loss of someone you love is the hardest thing to bear."

"But why did you deny knowing him?" I asked.

"I thought that you might be making enquiries on behalf of the French authorities, raking up all that business with his son. I thought he deserved peace," said the banker. "And then we heard of his death. Had I known when I spoke to you that he was dead, then I would have answered your question differently."

Wilson leaned forward in his seat, his notebook open on his knee. "Mr Renard," he asked, "how did you meet Mr Lagrange? When we first spoke of him, you said that you had known him for," Wilson glanced down at his notebook, "eight years. Where did you meet him again?"

The banker thought for a moment. "It was in Dover. I had gone there with a friend who was returning to France, to bid him farewell and to take the sea air for a few days, and Lagrange was at the dock, meeting a cargo from France. We fell to talking – two Frenchmen far from home – and found we had much in common."

"He spoke French, then," I asked.

"But of course," said Renard. "With a heavy accent, thanks to his English mother and a long absence from France." He stopped. "But this is a strange question, constable. Why should Monsieur Lagrange not speak French?"

"The poor man," said Martha as Wilson and I sat back in our chairs, stomachs full. "He must wonder whether there is anything left in this world that he can count on: his daughter is missing and wanted by the magistrates, his friend is not a French art buyer but an English robber..."

"And there is another matter that we did not raise with him, is there not, Wilson?"

Wilson walked over to his coat hanging on the wall and retrieved his notebook from its pocket. While his back was turned, I winked at Martha. Wilson pushed his plate aside and opened his notebook on the table.

"The absence of the chief clerk, Mr Greenwood," he read, then looked up at me and I nodded. "We know from what Constable Plank observed after the art auction on 20th February last that Mr Bonneville and Mr Greenwood were acquainted. And we know that Mr Greenwood was aware of the purchase of the miniature frames, and arranged for them to be divided between Bonneville and Lagrange. He said that it was on the instruction of Renard, which we assumed was the banker but we now know was Miss Renard." He closed his notebook. "So it seems that Mr Greenwood was involved too."

"And that is where we shall start tomorrow, Wilson," I said. "First thing, I would like you to go to Mr Freame's banking house in Cheapside and talk to the clerk, Stevenson. Ask him what he knows about Renard's clerks – he was full of useful information before."

Wilson stood and put on his coat. "Just me, sir? You do not want to go together?"

I shook my head. "I think you are ready to conduct your own interviews." Wilson beamed and then remembered that he was supposed to be a serious magistrates' constable and scratched his chin instead. "I will find something else to occupy me in the morning, and when you return to Great Marlborough Street we will share our findings and then make a report to Mr Conant. Go home now, and rest your mind in preparation – you did well today."

Martha sat on the edge of the bed, running her fingertips over her scalp looking for the pins she used to keep her hair neat during the day. When they were all removed, she shook her head and her curls tumbled loose over her shoulders – it was a sight of which I never tired. I reached across and lifted one of the curls, twisting it around my finger – there was a glint of silver in it these days, but that only made it all the more valuable to me.

"I am glad that you do not have to tie your hair in curling papers every night," I said. "It would be like sharing a pillow with a hedgehog."

Martha smiled and climbed into bed as I lifted the cover for her. "Did William do well today, Sam?" she asked. "It must have been difficult for him at the bank, surrounded by memories of happier times with Miss Renard." She settled against me, her head on my shoulder.

"To be honest, my dear, I have never heard him speak so eloquently. He was a little too demonstrative for my taste, but when dealing with a Frenchman, perhaps it was right," I said.

I felt my wife smile against my chest. "He listens a great deal, you know, does William. He listens to what you tell him, all of it. Sometimes he seems to be just sitting, but he's listening."

I sighed.

"What is it, Sam?" asked Martha, quick as ever to discern my mood.

"There is something else that troubles me, but I thought it best not to mention it to Wilson until I am more certain. We suspect that Sylvie Renard is capable of countenancing – of being involved in – the murder of Robert King. And Pierre Bonneville is also dead."

Martha turned to look up at me. "But you thought that was an accident – something he ate."

"And he was in the habit of eating meals prepared by Sylvie Renard." I licked my fingers, leaned over and snuffed out the candle. "Tomorrow morning I shall return to Craven Street and look through Miss Renard's room – I feel sure that there is more to learn about her."

CHAPTER THIRTY-FIVE

Meetings of minds

THURSDAY 5TH APRIL 1827

The next morning I returned alone to the bank in Craven Street. Again I knocked loudly at a locked door, and again the pale clerk let me in.

"Thank you, lad," I said. "What is your name?"

"Watkins, sir," he said quietly.

"And is Mr Greenwood returned?" I asked. Watkins shook his head; I was not surprised. "And Miss Renard?" Another shake of the head. "I shall go upstairs and call on Mr Renard."

As I walked past him towards the back of the bank, Watkins caught hold of my sleeve. "I think he needs to eat, sir – Mr Renard, that is. I went up yesterday evening before I left, to remind him that he should lock the door behind me, and he looked bad, sir. Crumpled." The clerk shook his head sadly. "He's been good to me, Mr Renard. There's not many would give me a chance, with a father on the rocks in the Marshalsea, but he did."

I stopped and looked at him. "Your father is in debtors' prison?" I asked.

"Not any longer, sir, God rest his soul. But thanks to the money I earn here, I repaid them all and now my mother and me, we've got a little lodging nearby, and we're making our way, sir." He stood up straighter.

"That is indeed something to be proud of, Watkins," I said. I knew for myself how hard it was to clamber your way out of the Marshalsea, with a father's debts like an anchor around your neck.

"I told my mother something of what happened here yesterday – not enough to worry her about my position, just that Mr Renard had had some sadness – and she has sent him some of her onion soup. Very fond of it, the French are, and she makes it special for him." Watkins darted off and reached under the bank counter, returning with a dish covered with a cloth. "Just a little warming, and it will be good as new." He handed the soup to me.

I climbed the stairs to the banker's apartment and, balancing the dish of soup carefully, knocked on the door.

"Come," called a weak voice, and I walked in to find Mr Renard sitting in the armchair where we had left him the day before. He looked up at me. "Constable Plank –

have you any news? Of Sylvie?" He sat forward in his seat, running his hands over his hair and then his beard. "But no – I can tell from your face." He slumped back again. "Forgive my appearance – I find that nothing matters as it once did."

I put the dish on the table. "From Mrs Watkins," I said, nodding at it. "She is concerned that you are not eating."

"And she is right but, between you and me, constable, her onion soup is not going to tempt me." The banker looked at me and tried a smile – it was a poor creature, but it was a start. "She knows that we French have a fondness for it, but her version, well, it is not the same. Not that I would ever tell her so."

I walked over to the banker and sat in one of the chairs that were still where I had placed them the day before. "It is a womanly trait, to comfort with food," I said. "My own wife had the selfsame idea and asked me to offer you this." I reached into my pocket and handed Renard a thick slice of walnut loaf wrapped in a napkin. "Very English, though, this – my own particular favourite."

"Then it is most generous of you both," said the banker, leaning over the napkin and quickly wiping a tear from his eye. "I have heated some water, if you'd care to…" He waved his hand in the direction of the kitchen, and I gave him a minute alone while I made some tea.

When I returned he offered me some of the loaf; I refused, and he made short work of the slice by himself, both of which facts I knew would please Martha.

"Now, constable, I know that you have not come here purely to deliver your wife's walnut loaf, delicious though it was," said Renard, carefully folding the napkin and handing it to me. "You want to know more about Sylvie, no?"

"If I am to understand her role in all of this, sir, and to determine whether she took part willingly, or was forced, yes, I need to know more about her," I said. "Your reaction yesterday told me that you knew nothing of any plans she had to go away, or of anything that was troubling her."

The banker shrugged. "She is a young woman of independent mind, constable – how much would she confide in her papa? But no, she did not seem troubled. I know that she and your young constable had a, shall we say, a dalliance, but that it came to an end. However, I would venture, sir, that he was more affected by it than she. An oddity, is it not, that the softer body of the woman conceals the more robust heart? It is we men whose hearts shatter more easily." He smiled sadly.

I nodded; I had often thought the same myself.

"Miss Renard gave Constable Wilson to understand that you did not approve of him," I said. "That you wished your daughter to marry a Frenchman, and that no English man would be good enough."

"Pah!" The banker looked surprised. "I have said no such thing; I have lived in England for many years, and we both know, constable, you and I, that there are good and bad men in every country. Perhaps Sylvie was seeking to spare your constable's feelings."

"Perhaps," I said. "Either way, you do not think that Miss Renard has gone away to recover from a broken heart?"

"No, constable, I do not," said the banker.

"And you can think of no other matter that might be relevant? You and she did not quarrel? She did not mention a friend in distress?"

At each of my questions the banker shook his head. "Constable Plank, I have sat here all night in this chair, trying to think of what might have caused Sylvie to leave. And I can think of nothing." He banged the arm of the chair. "Nothing."

I leaned forward and placed a hand on his arm. I knew how distressed I would be if Alice vanished without a word; how much worse it must be for a true father.

"I am sorry to upset you, sir," I said, "but if I am to help Miss Renard at all, I must ask these questions. And now, if you will permit, I would like to look at her room, to see if there is anything to hint at what has happened."

The banker nodded wordlessly and pointed to the door next to the kitchen.

As her father had said the day before, Miss Renard's room was in disarray. The cupboard door was open, with items pulled out and dropped carelessly onto the bed and the floor. Without knowing the extent of her wardrobe, I had no idea of how much she had taken with her, but Renard had said that some things had gone. The top of her dressing table was bare of brush, pins and all the other items I am told women need to arrange their hair. There was a strong smell of perfume, and on the floor by the dressing table was a broken scent bottle, suggesting that she had swept items from the surface in a hurry.

I glanced at her wash-stand and something caught my eye – a dark smudge in the bowl. I went closer and peered at it and then touched it with my fingertip: it was ash. Someone had burned something small – a scrap of paper perhaps. I looked behind the door for Miss Renard's coat, but the only thing hanging there was an apron and bonnet – perhaps the very ones she had been wearing when we first met. I put my hand into the pocket of the apron and felt a smooth container. I pulled it out and walked over to the window to look at it in better light. It was a glass phial of what looked like green paint pigment, mostly gone, with a cork in the top. I slipped it into my pocket, took a last look around the room and returned to the banker.

"Well, constable?" he asked.

"Is your daughter an artist, Mr Renard?" I asked. "Did she take lessons from Mr Bonneville, perhaps?"

Renard shook his head. "Sylvie is like me in that regard, constable: plenty of enthusiasm but no skill at all when it comes to drawing and painting. She says that we are instead that thing essential to all artists: the appreciative audience."

"Thank you, sir," I said, going over to the armchair. "I have all I need for now, and you can be sure that as soon as we know anything, I shall send word." I held out my hand and the banker shook it and then reached up with his other hand and grasped mine tightly.

"Please, constable, I beg of you: find my Sylvie. Whatever she has done, she is my little girl."

When I reached the foot of the stairs, Watkins jumped off his stool and came over to me.

"You can tell your mother, Watkins, that Mr Renard was very grateful for the soup, and that he has eaten," I said.

The clerk smiled and bowed as he held the door open for me. Once out in the street I looked up at the first floor window. Renard was there still, in his armchair, looking out. I raised a hand in farewell but his eyes were unseeing.

By the time I arrived at Great Marlborough Street I was chilled to the bone. Wilson was waiting in the back office, carefully reading his notebook with a pencil in his hand, so I knew that he had been putting marks against important details. He looked up at me and I shook my head.

"No sign of either Miss Renard or Mr Greenwood," I said, and then told him about the ash in the washbasin and the phial of green powder.

"A note, that she read and then burned?" he suggested.

"That was what I thought," I said. "And here's the phial." I handed it to him and he turned it to the light.

"The label is torn, but I can make out something... A – C – K – E."

"Ackermann's, I should imagine," I said, "on the Strand. They sell all manner of artists' materials – Miss Conant's paintbox came from there, and I daresay they sell the paints and pigments to go with it. But Miss Renard did not paint – I asked her father."

Wilson shrugged and passed me the phial. He looked down at his notebook. "I, on the other hand, have something very interesting to tell you." I sat down and put my hand to the pot of tea at Wilson's elbow; it was just warm enough and I poured myself a cup. "I spoke to Stevenson, and he said that after we showed an interest, he made it his business to get to know the junior clerk at Renard's banking house..."

"Watkins," I said.

Wilson checked his notebook. "George Watkins, yes. Anyway, Stevenson asked him a bit more about these so-called sympathies of his master, and we may have misunderstood."

"Misunderstood about the sympathies?" I asked.

Wilson shook his head. "Misunderstood about the master. Watkins told Stevenson that once a week, on Wednesday evenings, about eight or nine people would arrive at the banking house just as it was closing and go upstairs to the Renard apartment for what they called a 'meeting of minds'."

"What sort of people?" I asked. "Young? Old? French?"

"It varied a little, but all of those." Wilson leaned forward. "But that's not the interesting part. Watkins told Stevenson that Mr Renard sings baritone with a French choir, and that he attends a rehearsal once a week – on Wednesday evenings, leaving the bank a half-hour before it closes in order to reach the church in Soho on time."

I put my cup down. "So it is not Mr Renard holding these meetings of minds." I thought I knew the answer but I asked anyway. "Who does Watkins say is hosting these gatherings?"

"Miss Renard," said Wilson, "and Mr Greenwood."

"The daughter and the octogenarian clerk?" said Conant with amusement. "Are you sure?" He caught sight of the misery on Wilson's face, at the revelation of yet another way in which Miss Renard had fooled him, and spoke more seriously. "What I mean to say is that if we are to bring this matter before two of my colleagues on the bench without them thinking that I have taken leave of my senses, we must understand the connections."

"Indeed, sir," I said, nodding at Wilson, "and Constable Wilson has already sent a message to the clerk Watkins, asking him to come to the office tomorrow morning. I would rather not ask Mr Renard any more just at the moment; suggesting to him that his daughter is a revolutionary on top of everything else would be cruel."

"And so you think, Constable Wilson, that this Watkins may be able to tell you more about Mr Greenwood?" asked the magistrate.

"I do, sir, yes," said Wilson.

Just then the door opened and in came Miss Lily Conant, shaking rain from the hood of her cloak.

"Horrid weather," she said, smiling despite it. "Thank you, constable." This was directed at Wilson, who had hurried over to take the cloak from her shoulders. "I am sorry to interrupt but..." and here she caught sight of her father. "Oh papa, you have not even started to dress. We shall be late for la Signora Figlioni, which I daresay is your intent." She walked over and kissed her father's forehead before sitting on the low stool at his feet and looking up at me. "My father is to accompany me to a recital at the Royal Opera House by the famous Italian soprano la Signora Figlioni, but I suspect that he is doing everything in his power to avoid what he calls the dreadful squawking."

"You must forgive him, Miss Conant," I said. "He has been delayed by our business. One minute more, and we will release you both to the squawking." I took the green phial from my pocket and handed it to the magistrate. "I found this in Miss Renard's room," I said. "It is probably nothing, but she was not an artist herself so had no cause to have it. Although we do know that she was acquainted with several artists, so perhaps one of them charged her with buying a replacement."

Lily Conant held out her hand. "May I see that, papa?" she asked. She studied the phial. "It is from Ackermann's, Constable Plank," she said. "I have the same label on my pigments. But you must be careful with this one. Emerald green. It is a wonderful colour, very rich, but – what is the word? – unstable. In powder like this, it is safe enough, but mix it with other substances, or heat it, and it becomes deadly poisonous. It releases arsenic."

"Good heavens, Lily," said Conant, reaching out hurriedly to take the phial from his daughter. "Where on earth do you learn such things?"

"Monsieur Bonneville," replied Lily. "He went through our paintboxes with us, telling us all about the colours and their formulations. It was very interesting. I shall miss him."

I looked at Wilson. His white face told me that he had reached the same realisation as I had. Arsenic poisoning can take several days to kill a man, during which time he will experience terrible twisting pain in the stomach, vomiting and diarrhoea – the very symptoms that the maid had described being suffered by Pierre Bonneville.

CHAPTER THIRTY-SIX

A dog with a bone

FRIDAY 6TH APRIL 1827

The next morning George Watkins was, as befits a bank clerk, prompt in his attendance at Great Marlborough Street at eight o'clock. Wilson met him in the front office and brought him through to the back, where I was waiting. He sat and folded his hands neatly in his lap, and I enquired after Mr Renard.

"He is no better, sir," said the clerk sadly. "My mother sends food every day, but I think that he does not eat it. He pretends that he does, and the dishes are empty, but he does not care for himself."

"Mr Renard has had a great many shocks in recent days," I said. "Now, Mr Watkins, we wanted to ask you about Mr Greenwood. Have you known him long?"

Watkins nodded. "Ever since I joined the banking house. Nearly four years now."

"And what do you know of Mr Greenwood's life outside the banking house?" I asked. "Does he have any family?"

"He is a widower – has been for as long I have known him, and I think for some years before that. He does not talk of his children, but I know he must have at least one because he talks a great deal about his late grandson, Charles."

I leafed back through my notebook. "When I first met Mr Renard," I said, "he too mentioned that Mr Greenwood had a grandson – died at Toulouse."

"That's right," said Watkins. "Mr Greenwood talks about it a lot – like a dog with a bone." He flushed. "Oh, I am sorry, sir: I do not mean to be disrespectful to Mr Greenwood. All I meant was that he often refers to his grandson's death – the sheer waste of it all, he says."

Wilson cleared his throat. "Excuse me, sir," he said, "but what is the significance of Toulouse?"

"The Battle of Toulouse?" I replied. "1814 – I daresay your teachers tried to tell you a little of the Peninsular Wars." Wilson nodded. "Toulouse is in southern France, and was the site of one of the final battles between us, in alliance with the Spanish and the Portuguese, and the French Imperial armies. There were many dead on both sides. That is terrible enough, but what is infinitely worse is that the whole battle was entirely unnecessary, as Napoleon had surrendered four days earlier. So I can understand how Mr Greenwood, losing a loved one in such circumstances, would consider it a waste."

Watkins nodded. "He says," he dropped his voice and leaned forward, "that it was the fault of the commanders, that they condemned thousands to their deaths without a moment's thought, and that had they done their jobs properly and sent word of the surrender to the men in Toulouse, his grandson would still be alive. Apparently he died only a week after his seventeenth birthday."

"Indeed," I said, glancing at Wilson. "You told Constable Wilson that once a week, on Wednesday evenings, Miss Renard and Mr Greenwood host meetings in the apartment above the banking house. Meetings of minds, I believe you said."

"That's what Mr Greenwood calls them, yes," said the clerk.

"How many people attend these meetings, Mr Watkins?" I asked.

"It varies a little, but about eight or ten people, I would say, as well as Miss Renard and Mr Greenwood."

"And do you recognise any of them?" I asked. "I mean, apart from them becoming familiar to you through regular attendance at the meetings."

"There's Mr Bonneville – he comes most weeks," said Watkins. "He is easy to recognise, with that hair and those artistic clothes." He smiled, and then his face fell. "I mean, he was easy to recognise. I liked Mr Bonneville; he was always polite to me and enquired after my health."

"But others are not polite?" I asked.

"Mostly they nod at me as I open the door for them, but do not speak." He hesitated.

"Go on, Mr Watkins," I said.

"But there is one man I do not like." The clerk shook his head. "He attends most weeks, and I do not like his manner."

"He is rude to you?" I asked.

"Not to me, no – he ignores me. It is his manner with Mr Greenwood that I do not like. He is abrupt with him, almost rough at times, hurrying him across the banking hall. Once I heard him call Mr Greenwood an old fool, and I did not like that."

"Do you know his name, this man?" I asked.

Watkins shook his head. "But he's English, definitely, not French. And aged about, well, older than you, sir, but not old."

I smiled. "About in his mid fifties, then. Were you ever curious about these meetings, Mr Watkins?" I asked.

The clerk shrugged. "I once asked Mr Greenwood about them, and he said that they were philosophical discussions between people interested in Utopia. I looked it up: an ideal society based on equality and the common good."

"And you were never invited to attend?"

"Me, sir?" The clerk smiled. "I do not seek an ideal society; I seek only to make my way in this one, and my mother needs me home promptly at the end of the day."

"Quite right," I said. "But these meetings are always held on Wednesday evenings, when Mr Renard is away from home. Did he know about the meetings, do you think?"

Watkins looked down at his hands and shook his head.

"And you did not tell him?" I asked.

The clerk shook his head again. "She asked me not to – Miss Renard." He looked at me, a blush on his cheeks. "And I promised her that I would not."

"She can be very charming when it suits her," said Wilson, and I raised a warning eyebrow at him.

It was clear that the clerk was not involved with these meetings or those who attended, and he would need to be on his way if he were to reach work on time – although I doubted whether Mr Renard would even notice whether his banking house opened or stayed closed.

"Thank you, Mr Watkins," I said. "You have been of great help. All we need from you now is Mr Greenwood's address."

"Any observations?" I asked Wilson as we walked the short distance to Rupert Street.

"Well, I do not think that we need to worry about Mr Watkins," said Wilson.

"You think him an innocent in these matters?" I asked as we stepped into the street to avoid a bucket of mucky water thrown into the gutter by a maid.

"Yes," said Wilson. "He should perhaps have told Mr Renard about the meetings, but then we have all done foolish things when bidden by a woman."

I smiled to myself at his world-weary tone, so recently acquired. "Indeed we have," I agreed.

"I am more interested in this Englishman who attends the meetings and was abrupt with Mr Greenwood," said Wilson.

We arrived at the address that Watkins had given us; it was a shop with rooms above. "Jean Armand", said the neat lettering over the crowded window, "Purveyor of Musical Instruments and Sheet Music". I pushed open the door and a bell sounded, summoning a gentleman from the back room. He was advanced in years, small, with bright eyes in an intelligent face. He was wearing a long apron over his clothes, and there was sawdust in his hair.

"Good morning, sir," I said.

"Gentlemen," he said, bowing so that sawdust shook onto the floor in front of him. He spotted it and smiled at me. "I am repairing a sadly neglected violoncello, and there is much sanding and polishing to be done." He was French, of course. "But you are," he came closer and looked at us more carefully, "officers of the law, not musicians".

"We are indeed, sir," I said. "Constable Plank and Constable Wilson, of Great Marlborough Street. And we are come to call on Mr Greenwood."

"Ah, le pauvre," said the shopkeeper, shaking his head and setting free more sawdust. "He is upstairs." He pointed to the ceiling. "You can go up here." He walked over to the curtain in the corner of the shop and pulled it aside to reveal a narrow staircase. "But I think he is near the end, constables." He crossed himself. "I wait for his son to return, but nothing – not since Tuesday. It is cruel for a man to die alone, so my wife and I, we sit with him when we can. She is there now, Madame Armand. Please." Mr Armand indicated the staircase and Wilson and I went upstairs.

Above the shop was a small apartment of three rooms. In the largest, an elderly woman sat on a chair beside the bed, a piece of needlework in her hands. She looked up at us as we walked in and put her finger to her lips.

"We have come to see Mr Greenwood," I said quietly.

She nodded and beckoned us closer, then stood to offer me her chair.

"You find his son?" she asked in broken English. I shook my head. "Soon," she whispered, "too late."

"I understand, madame," I said. "We will not stay long."

Madame Armand reached over and patted Greenwood's hand, then left the room.

I sat in the chair. "Mr Greenwood," I said, "can you hear me?"

The old man in the bed stirred and opened his eyes. "Hear you, and see you," he said. "Why yes, Constable Plank, is it not?"

"It is, sir, and Constable Wilson," I replied. "I am sorry to find you like this."

"Don't be ridiculous, constable," said Greenwood, and then wheezed as he struggled to get his breath. I leaned over him and hauled him a little more upright, pushing a pillow into the small of his back. "I am eighty years old, nearly eighty-one – how much longer would you have me live?" He took a deeper breath. "Watkins told you where to find me, I suppose."

"Mr Watkins is concerned for you, as is Mr Renard," I said. "Our interest is rather less benign."

"Well, you're too late, constable, benign or not." He smiled at me, but it was a twisted smile. "Those two downstairs think that Thomas – my son – will come back, but he will not. No: by now they will be in France, carrying the cause with them."

"They?" I asked, knowing the answer but hoping that I was wrong.

"Thomas and Sylvie – they wanted to take me with them, but what use would I be to them now?" The old man gestured to indicate his ailing body. "I have done all I can, bringing them together with others who share their aims and are willing to make whatever sacrifice is necessary."

"Raising money through the fraudulent sale of miniatures," I added.

"Ah, that was Thomas's idea – a clever one, I thought – and I was happy, no, proud to help," said the old man.

"And your role was to act as go-between, for messages between Houseman, Bonneville and their customers?" I asked. "Using Mr Renard's name to give it respectability?"

He nodded. "Quite so. It gave me satisfaction to know that England's wealthiest families were contributing money to our cause – the irony is pleasing, is it not, constable?"

"Supporting an armed uprising against the ruling classes is not pleasing to my mind, no, Mr Greenwood," I said.

"The ruling classes!" Greenwood spat the words at me. "Centuries of inbreeding and privilege, and what do we have? Idiots with no concern for anyone but themselves. They take from the rest of us – our skills, our ideas, our sweat, our children – and leave us with nothing."

"While you in your turn, Mr Greenwood, have left Mr Renard with nothing. In your pursuit of – what did Watkins call it? – Utopia, you and your like-minded friends have murdered one customs officer and severely injured another."

"Unthinking servants of those ruling classes of yours," said Greenwood.

I ignored him and continued. "You have murdered Louis Rambert – a blameless man – and Pierre Bonneville."

"Rambert would not do as he was told," said Greenwood.

"And Bonneville?" I asked.

Greenwood smiled his twisted smile again. "Ah, so you do not know everything after all, Constable Plank." He looked away for a moment and then back at me. "Still, I suppose it does not matter now. Pierre Bonneville was a spy, constable." I remembered the man we saw leaving Bonneville's studio, and the man who picked up Bonneville's note in Covent Garden – not customers, then, but his channel for passing on information. "A clever choice: who would have thought of recruiting someone so flamboyant, so very noticeable as a spy? When we found out, we had no other option. Sylvie begged to be allowed to do it – said that he trusted her. I think she was pleased to do something so important for the cause."

By now I was sick of that wretched phrase, 'the cause', but I kept myself under control. "And you have broken the heart and home of Pascal Renard," I continued, "a good Frenchman who sought nothing more than to make a life in England for himself and his daughter."

"Renard is a fool – he signed anything I put in front of him," said Greenwood, with a wheeze that was meant as a laugh. "And she will be my daughter soon, anyway. Oh yes: she and Thomas will wed as soon as they reach France. The child will be born there, into – God willing – a better world."

I heard a sharp intake of breath behind me. I stood and looked down at the dying man. "I think, sir," I said calmly, "you presume too much if you seek to recruit God to the cause."

After taking our leave of the Armands, Wilson and I walked out into the bustle of Soho, and I welcomed its distractions. Wilson had been dealt some heavy blows and there was little I could do except bear the knowledge with him. We reached the end of Rupert Street and I turned left to head back to Great Marlborough Street, but Wilson stopped.

"If you don't mind, sir," he said, "I will leave you here."

I looked at him with concern. "She had her head turned, you know, with all of this talk of Utopia. When you are surrounded by people with deformed morals, your own sense of what is right and wrong can become unbalanced."

He nodded and bit his lip. "I just wonder whether, if I had noticed that about her," he said hesitantly, "we could have stopped any of this. The murders. The girls at Mrs Plank's school."

"If you had noticed, would I have believed you?" I asked. "And if I had believed you, could we have convinced Mr Conant?" I put a hand on his arm. "You are a young constable, with decades of service ahead of you. How can you expect to know everything? I met Miss Renard and I suspected nothing, even with all of my years in uniform. What you must do – what we all must do – is learn from every experience. That is what makes a good constable, Wilson, and you will be a very good constable."

Wilson looked down at the ground and then up at me with a watery smile.

"Thank you, sir."

"Now," I said in encouraging tones, "my advice to you is to go for a long walk, with a stiff drink at the end of it, and think about what has happened so that it does not disturb your sleep. And tomorrow, we start afresh."

"I shall, sir: a walk, and then a drink. I think I shall call in at the Blue Boar – one of little Martha's smiles will soon see me right."

"Little Martha's smiles," said big Martha, with a broad smile of her own. "They are a tonic, it's true, but so is her mother. Alice is very calming, I always find: gentle, and quiet, with a deep warmth to her heart. A good contrast to Miss Sylvie Renard." My wife sniffed.

"You are match-making again, my love," I said. "If Wilson and Alice like each other well enough, they will find that out in their own time."

"But it does not hurt to put them in each other's way," said Martha, and I knew better than to argue the point. "Poor William," she said, holding my shirt up to the fire and shaking it out. "There: good as new." She reached into her mending basket for the next item – one of little Martha's baby bonnets, by the look of it. "Martha has outgrown it," she explained, catching my glance, "and if I unpick the lace, it will do for Mrs Horne's little boy." She laid the bonnet in her lap and set to with her sharp sewing scissors. "So this Thomas Greenwood was at the centre of things, you think?"

I nodded. "There were two people we had not identified: the man who went with Rambert to arrange his lodging with Mrs Anderson, and the man who led the attack on Ben. From what I saw of the man in the vaults, and from Mrs Anderson's description – an Englishman a little older than I am – they could both be Thomas Greenwood."

"And he has made good his escape, over to France," said Martha. "I am sorry, Sam." I smiled and she narrowed her eyes at me. "What is it, Sam?" she asked. "Is there something you have not told me?" She laid down her scissors.

"As I listened to Mr Greenwood – the father – talking of his blessed cause, and of Utopia, I had to admit to a certain sympathy," I said. Martha's eyes widened. "No, not for revolution, but for his anger at the futility of war. We beat Napoleon, it's true, but at what cost? Thousands of our men dead, many more thousands come back from the wars with no skills beyond killing and no hope of employment. No hope of anything, it must seem to many of them."

Martha sighed. "I know: I sometimes look at Wilson and thank God that he was born too late."

"But one good thing has come out of it all: co-operation. You remember I told you of the Congress of Vienna?" I asked. "When the nations agreed on post-war reparations and division of land?" Martha nodded. "Well, they also agreed on co-operation in criminal matters. And so tomorrow I will be sending a request to

France for assistance in locating and arresting Thomas Greenwood and Sylvie Renard. It may come to nothing but I am hopeful."

"You see, Sam," said Martha, picking up her scissors once more, "I told you that learning French would be useful."

And as I watched my wife at her sewing, the curls escaping from her cap and catching the firelight, I wondered how I could ever have considered Sylvie Renard's hair anything like Martha's. One was good and true and decent, and the other merely an eye-catching but shallow copy.

CHAPTER THIRTY-SEVEN

Regard

THURSDAY 12TH APRIL 1827

"Constable Plank," said Henri Causon warmly, holding out his hand. "I did wonder whether I might see you again."

"Indeed?" I said, taking the seat he indicated.

"Oh yes. The community of dealers in French art here in London is small, and there has been much talk of an interesting trade in miniatures. As you can imagine, we have all been examining our own collections very carefully, to make sure that they are genuine. I am relieved to report that my pieces are all from France. Although none, hélas, is quite as charming as that little one you brought me when we first met – Elizabeth, I believe you called her?"

"I had hoped that you would remember her," I said. I reached into my pocket and took out the tiny portrait, wrapped as always in the softest of my handkerchiefs that Martha could find. I handed it to the art dealer and he carefully unfolded the fabric.

"Ah," he said gently. "Even lovelier than I had remembered."

"When I first brought her to you, I could tell you nothing of how she was found, but now I can. She was clutched tightly – like this," I made a fist to demonstrate, "in the hand of an artist who had been murdered. We think – although we have no proof at all – that she was his grand-daughter. Other paintings were taken from his studio, but he died to hold on to this one."

"How sad," said the dealer, gazing down at the little portrait. "Certainly it was painted with great love for its subject."

"Mr Causon, Mr Conant – the magistrate – has sent me here with a proposition for you." The dealer looked up reluctantly. "The true owner of the miniature is dead. It would not be appropriate for anyone involved in the matter, such as Mr Conant himself, or me, to keep hold of it – there might be accusations of corruption. On the other hand, we have all grown very fond of Elizabeth, and we feel that her grandfather would rest more easily knowing that she was loved and appreciated. In short, Mr Conant asks if you would like to acquire the miniature."

The dealer looked down again at the portrait cradled in his palm. "Constable," he said, "I should like nothing better."

"Mr Conant has written down a price that he feels would be fair," I said, handing Causon a folded piece of paper. "If acceptable to you, the money would be given to an establishment with which my wife is concerned, for the education of young girls who have had an unfortunate start in life."

The dealer looked at the paper and nodded. "This is a very fair price, constable, and I am sure that Elizabeth's grandfather would be pleased to know that the proceeds of his work are going to assist such an admirable enterprise. If you could wait, I have some funds in my study." Causon rose, and I stood too.

"Mr Causon," I said. "Mr Conant did ask me to explain that there was one condition attached to the sale. He would very much prefer you to keep Elizabeth for your personal collection, and not to add her to your stock for sale to others. It is an unusual request, I know, but he has a much loved daughter himself and can be sentimental in such things."

"Then he and I are in complete accord on the matter. I could not bear to part with her myself; this exquisite child will have a permanent home here."

Ten minutes later Causon returned with a letter addressed to Conant.

"I have enclosed the agreed payment," he said, "and my personal assurance to Mr Conant that the miniature will stay with me and not be offered for sale."

"Thank you, sir," I said, taking the letter and slipping it into my pocket. Conant had been right in his estimation of Causon, and as we were walking towards the door I decided that I too would put my trust in this man. "Mr Causon," I said, "my wife and I have been married for twenty-five years."

"My felicitations, sir, to you both." Causon stopped and smiled but looked puzzled.

"I am not a man of lavish display, Mr Causon," I continued, "but I love my wife very much. And I saw the great pleasure she took in looking at that miniature – how she enjoyed having something beautiful to admire. I could not offer her Elizabeth, but I think it would be fitting for me to mark the occasion of our anniversary with something," I waved my arm to take in the crowded cabinets and walls of the drawing room, "something of note. You are obviously a man of experience in these matters, and it would be of great assistance to me if you could suggest..." I shook my head despairingly. "I know my wife, sir, but I know nothing of this world of beautiful objects."

"Then we are a good match, constable, and between us we shall fix on the right thing." The Frenchman led me back to the armchairs and we both sat down.

"Your wife, sir," he began, "is she very feminine – taken with pretty little things and dainty items – or more practical in her tastes?" I stared at him mutely. He tried again. "Her night-dress, let us say: does it have much lace at the collar and hem?"

I felt myself redden slightly, but I could see the method of his approach. "A little lace, yes, but Martha – Mrs Plank – places more importance on the quality of the fabric than on its adornments."

"Perhaps that is why she chose to marry a constable," said Causon. "And it is almost certainly why that constable still values and admires her so many years later." He stood and walked over to a glass-topped cabinet, looking at its contents for a few moments before saying, "Ah," quietly to himself and sliding out the drawer. He picked up a small item and brought it over to me, placing it in my open palm. It was a ring, quite simple and yet substantial and obviously of excellent quality. Around the plain gold band were held six coloured stones: two large central ones flanked by four smaller ones.

"It is known as a regard ring," said Causon. "Each of the stones provides a letter to spell out the word, so you have a ruby, then an emerald, a garnet, an amethyst, another ruby, and a diamond. Regard."

I turned the ring to the light and imagined Martha's surprise on seeing it. Causon had chosen perfectly. Regard. Not as showy or as brilliant as passion, to be sure, but much more lasting.

Glossary

Banbury tale – a roundabout, nonsensical story

Bandog – a fierce type of mastiff dog, bred to guard and protect

Breeched – when a young boy was taken out of unisex petticoats and dressed in trousers, or breeches, for the first time, he was said to be breeched (note: not the same as *well breeched*)

Blockademan – a customs officer, charged particularly with stopping smuggling, and most commonly used in east Kent

Cato Street conspiracy – this was a plot by more than twenty men, named after their meeting place in London, to murder the Prime Minister Lord Liverpool and his en-

tire cabinet in February 1820; there was a police inform-
ant, the plot was discovered, and five conspirators were
executed while five more were transported to Australia

Cheapside – to come at something by way of Cheapside
is to buy it cheap, to pay less than it is worth

Cocket – a receipt issued to the captain of a ship, showing that his cargo has been inspected and that all relevant
duties have been calculated and paid

Constable – an officer working for a magistrates' court,
whose main duty is to arrest people named in warrants
issued by the magistrates

Duds – clothes

Easement – prisoners were often manacled and then
chained to staples in the floor; payment to the gaoler
would permit the fitting of lighter manacles (known as
easement of the manacles) or their removal altogether

Gambling hell – an establishment purely for gambling,
unlike the more respectable gentlemen's clubs, which offered gambling as one of a number of diversions for their
members alongside, for example, dining and lectures

Garnish – by payment of garnish to his gaoler, a prisoner could secure comforts such as candles and soap

Gentleman of the road – a highwayman, a highway robber

Greenhead – an inexperienced young man

Gull – one who is deceived or cheated (gulled), usually
at the gaming table

Hempen widow – a woman whose husband was hanged

Henry Fauntleroy – the banker whose story is the subject of the first Sam Plank novel, "Fatal Forgery"

Jarvey – driver of a hackney coach

Jug-bitten – drunk

Ladybird – a woman of easy virtue, a prostitute

Leipzig – the Battle of Leipzig took place over four days in October 1813, at Leipzig in Saxony, and involved nearly 600,000 men; the coalition armies of Russia, Prussia, Austria and Sweden decisively defeated Napoleon's French army

Lighter – a flat-bottomed barge, used for transporting cargo between larger vessels and the shore

Lighterman – a man who pilots a lighter on the river

Mercer – a merchant who deals in textiles

On dit – gossip

On the rocks – in debt

Pepperbox – a repeating, handheld firearm with three or more barrels grouped around a central axis, thus enabling several shots to be fired in quick (albeit, in 1827, hand-rotated) succession

Peterloo Massacre – on 16 August 1819, at St Peter's Field in Manchester, a crowd of up to 80,000 people gathered to demand the reform of parliamentary representation; local magistrates ordered the military to disperse the crowd, and when cavalrymen charged the unarmed gathering with sabres drawn, fifteen people were killed and as many as seven hundred wounded

Puff – in gambling clubs, puffs were employed to act as decoys, apparently playing and winning with high stakes, to entice customers to spend more

Puff guts – a fat man

Purblind – dim-sighted

Rum cull – a rich fool, easily cheated by anyone

Skeleton suit – an outfit worn by small boys once they were *breeched* (put into trousers), consisting of a tight jacket buttoned to high-waisted trousers, worn with a white shirt underneath

Square toes – an old man, as they are fond of wearing comfortable shoes with room around the toes

Tide-waiter – a customs officer who would board incoming vessels arriving on the high tide and check that they tied up at the appointed place; a tide-waiter would join London-bound vessels at Greenwich and make sure that the cargo was not unloaded on an isolated jetty out of sight, to evade duty, and to keep the tide-waiter honest, he was overseen by a tide surveyor

Tyburn Tree – the nickname for a scaffold erected during the reign of Elizabeth I at Tyburn in London, near the present-day site of Marble Arch, and often used to hang highwaymen; it was made of a wooden triangle supported by three legs and designed so that several felons could be hanged at once, and was last used in 1783, after which London's principal place of execution was moved to Newgate

Well breeched – with plenty of money in the pocket

Whippersnapper – a small, lively boy

Thank you for reading this book. If you liked what you read, please would you leave a short review on the site where you purchased it, or recommend it to others? Reviews and recommendations are not only the highest compliment you can pay to an author; they also help other readers to make more informed choices about purchasing books.

ABOUT THE AUTHOR

Susan Grossey graduated from Cambridge University in 1987 and since then has made her living from crime. She advises financial institutions and others on money laundering – how to spot criminal money, and what to do about it. She has written many non-fiction books on the subject of money laundering, as well as contributing monthly articles to the leading trade magazine and maintaining a popular anti-money laundering blog.

Her first work of fiction was the inaugural book in the Sam Plank series, "Fatal Forgery". "The Man in the Canary Waistcoat" was her second novel, "Worm in the Blossom" her third, and now "Portraits of Pretence" is her fourth. Three more Sam Plank mysteries are planned, to complete the series of seven.

Made in the USA
Charleston, SC
31 October 2016